CYBERIA

Monkey See, Monkey Don't

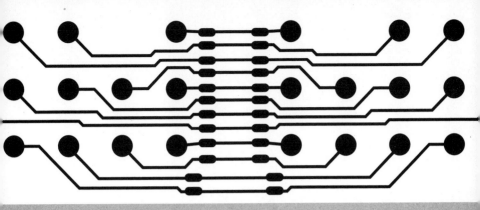

CHRIS LYNCH
CYBERIA
Monkey See, Monkey Don't

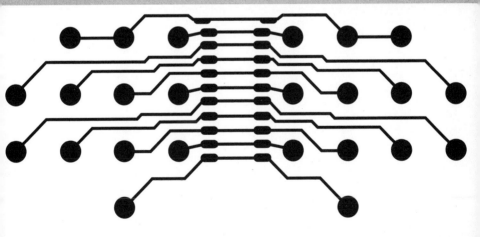

SCHOLASTIC PRESS
NEW YORK

Library of Congress Cataloging-in-Publication Data

Lynch, Chris.
    Monkey see, monkey don't / Chris Lynch. — 1st ed.
        p. cm. — (Cyberia ; #2)
    Summary: In a future where electronic surveillance has taken the place of love, young Zane uses technology to talk to animals and battles an evil veterinarian who is working on a new device to control animal movement and speech and plans to use Zane's dog as his first test case.
    ISBN-13: 978-0-545-02794-6 (hardcover : alk. paper)
    ISBN-10: 0-545-02794-2 (hardcover : alk. paper)
[1. Human-animal communication — Fiction. 2. Dogs — Fiction. 3. Animal rescue — Fiction. 4. Veterinarians — Fiction. 5. Technology — Fiction. 6. Electronic surveillance — Fiction. 7. Science fiction.] I. Title. II. Title: Monkey see, monkey don't.
    PZ7.L979739Mo 2009
    [Fic] — dc22
                            2009013564

    10 9 8 7 6 5 4 3 2 1   09 10 11 12 13

                Printed in the U.S.A.   23
                First edition, November 2009

            The text type was set in Adobe Caslon.
            Book design by Christopher Stengel

To my brother Brian — he's better than
everybody else, but . . . oh wait, he
already knows that.

He is pretty great, though.

SHORT, CARPETED ROAD
TO FREEDOM

The problem was that I did something.

I went pretty much a lifetime without, you know, *doing* anything, and then I did something, and it was chaos. I got in trouble, incarcerated, incapacitated for two months that were longer than the previous one hundred and thirty that I had lived (combined). I did something, and made some people angry, made myself a serious and scary enemy, and changed my life profoundly and irreversibly.

What a rush. I cannot wait to do another something.

"Have you learned your lesson, Zane?"

"Are you joking? Of course I've learned my lesson. Whatever that lesson might happen to be, I'm sure I've learned it. I've learned that lesson, and all the other lessons, since learning lessons is all I have been allowed to do for the last two months. If I were a tick, and lessons were blood, I would be splattered all over the room by now. How's that for lesson learning?"

"Hnnn. Not sure we're hearing quite what we had hoped to hear today, attitudewise."

That's my father talking. That Voice is raining down over me as I lie on my bed, greeting the first day of my soon-to-be-continued life. I've been canned for two months because of my behavior, and today is supposed to be the can opener. I can't see him, but That Voice is everywhere.

I can see my mother, though. My mother is primarily a Face, while my father is almost entirely a Voice. Her face is on a big screen, right next to another big screen that is replaying a report she did earlier this morning. She still has her hair, clothes, and makeup done exactly the same as when she was on the air, so the only difference between professional Newsmama and domestic Newsmama is the content of the report. And the slight motherly edge reserved for me and not her legions of televisual followers.

"Maybe you wouldn't mind a little extra time on your own before you're released, young man?" she says. "To perhaps look a little deeper into yourself and your actions?"

"Well, maybe that's a good idea," I say.

I am bluffing, of course. If I look any deeper into myself, I'll be sitting on my face.

They can't keep me locked up any longer anyway, since this is not your ordinary, kid-sent-to-his-room jailing. It's the real thing. My room is electronically bolted. I can

2

only leave at certain times, for appointments, chores, and other guardian-approved actions. If I am not in my room 23.3 hours of the day, alarms start going off all over the place and we get a visit from the authorities.

Like I said, I made some people mad.

But it all ends this morning at eight o'clock. Fifteen more minutes and I am sprung.

"I do hope this new feisty attitude of yours is just a result of being cooped up for two months, Zane," my mother says. "It would be a shame if we lost that sweet and lovely boy you were before all this craziness happened."

"Sweet and lovely is dead, mother. I killed him myself."

"Zane," That Voice booms. He really is booming. My father doesn't show anger a lot — he just gets extra layers of serious. Right now he sounds like he's gargling hot lava. "This is not going to be tolerated. If you speak in that tone to your mother again . . ."

It is kind of funny when That Voice — a voice that carries so much authority it can make *God* sit up straight — trails off. Because he can't really finish his sentence. Because he doesn't really do anything about anything.

I know how that feels. I was like that, before everything happened.

"Sorry, Dad? You were saying something?"

He's only three doors down. He could say that if I don't stop sassing my mother, he will come marching right down that hall and . . . wait fifteen minutes for my door to electronically open, then give me the good cuffing around I deserve. He could say that, and he wouldn't really be out of line since I was being kind of jerky to my perfectly adequate Newsmama, who very nearly won a local daytime Emmy award once. I'd even kind of respect him for it.

But he tanks.

"So . . . what are you going to do with your first big day of freedom?" he asks.

"Oh, I'm feeling a little run-down, so I thought mostly I'd lie around."

"Well, do pace yourself," says my mother, taking me seriously. Remarkable. "You don't want to get all wiped out on your first day."

"Right, Zany," Dad says. "That's good advice. Listen, I've got to get back to work here, so have a great day, and keep me posted."

"Posted you'll be, Dad."

"Eat a good breakfast, son," my mother says as her smiling, waving self fades from the live screen. Her serious, informational self remains on the other screen, but I have muted her. Muting people is so powerful.

Now, as I lie here awaiting the eight o'clock liberation, I feel weirdly crummy. I feel bad for being a talking zoink to my parents. They're not bad, they're neutral, and deserve a general sort of respect. My talking-to-real-people skills have truly gotten worse during my lockup. Things will improve. I will improve.

Then, the sound.

I can really hear it as the seconds tick off till my release. I have my Gizzard™ strapped cool macho to my upper arm, and I've already fitted the noodle into my ear, the earpiece that brings my whole technological world into my head. So when it all comes back online, I am ready. Ten and nine and eight and the rest, and it's thunderous as I realize just how much I'm wanting this, and three and two and I love the huge sound this is going to make as all the stuff I have been denied snaps back to life and into my arms and holy smokes am I feeling it now, my *power* returning to me. . . .

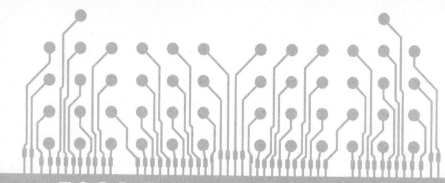

ZANE THE PLANE, READY FOR TAKEOFF

Scratch.

The clock has hit eight A.M.

Scratch.

I thought it would be like a boom, or a whoosh.

Scratch-scratch.

I get up off my bed, walk to the door, and check it. It opens.

Hugo is standing there. He stares at me wicked, like, "Two whole months, and *that's* how quick you answer the door?"

He doesn't say it, but I know that's how he would say it.

I wish he could say it.

"Hi, buddy," I say.

I wait, I wait, I wait, to hear him say something back. He has been here the whole time — except that unlike me he could come and go and have, y'know, a life. The whole two months, he kept me company, being a dog, being a silent friend. But he has not been talking to me. And I just figured, with my life coming back to me today, with the e-locks popping off and the communications and freedoms popping back on, that maybe, just possibly, the end of my sentence would bring back everything that has been taken away from me.

"Hi, buddy," I say.

He stares at me. He is a world-class staremaster, and gets his whole self into it. He's all white, with the legs of a small dog, the torso of a medium one, and the head of something a lot bigger than me. He tilts that head in just the way — piercing black eyes emerging from snowy mountain of skull — that makes me feel a little pathetic, then he walks past me into the room. Hugo ain't talking.

So the freedom feels a little less than it might have, because I don't know quite what world I'm walking back into now. I need to find out what's out there, find out what I've missed and what's in store for me. Dr. Gristle is the man who accidentally gave me a talking Hugo to begin with, and he is the man who very deliberately took him away again. He is the master of giveth-taketh right now, and he certainly isn't prepared to see me stroll back onto the scene, after I was such a menace to his idea of society.

I go to my old computer and fire it up. I check out my Gizzard™, and see how it's working. All around me, my room is fuzzing and buzzing in a way it hasn't in a long time because my communications have been practically on lockdown. I could communicate with my parents, receive and return my schoolwork, and check my temperature on the big board, but that's about it.

Now it's all unlocking, and I can't believe how excited I'm getting.

"Better watch it. That heart rate is looking kind of *scary* up there."

Gizzard™ is already messaging me.

I look to my vital statistics monitor screen and find that my heart is racing a bit. That's good, since by the end of my boring incarceration I think it was beating about three times an hour.

"And you might want to get outside for a walk or something. All this lying around has you looking rather portly."

"Hey, shut up, Gizzard™," I say, grabbing a small roll of fat at my belt line. "It's not a lot of fat — and anyway, when did you become a personal trainer?"

I cannot believe that five minutes after regaining my status as master of my universe, I am taking life-coach commands from my handheld.

Only ... I replay it in my head, in my ear. It isn't Gizzard™, it's —

"Hiya, fatty, welcome back online."

The accent, and attitude, are distinctly Yorkshire.

I whip around from the screens to encounter dirty, rotten Hugo sitting right behind me. He's got his back to me, like I'll be fooled by that.

I grab him up, wrestle him onto his back, and pin him to the floor.

"Why didn't you answer when I tried to talk to you?" I ask.

"Nobody calls me *buddy*. Have you ever noticed that every single dog named *Buddy* is a Frisbee-chasing idiot, usually wearing a neckerchief? I assumed you were talking to somebody else, Bozo."

Imagine, I've been waiting sixty-one whole days to have this conversation.

"Nice talking to you, too," I say.

"How's it feel to be back online?"

"Great. I can't wait to get caught up. For starters, how'd you get your voice back?"

"Not entirely sure. Your pal Gristle came by yesterday, shot something into me — yet another chip, I assume. I didn't have any idea what he was up to, since nobody ever consults me. He's done it so many times now I figured he likes to drop by every once in a while just to stab me."

"Well, I am sorry about that. But I'm glad we can talk."

"Yes, it is good that we can talk. Friends need to tell each other things. Like right now I have to tell you to put on some sneakers because we have to get your flabby self out for a run around the park."

"Shut up," I tell him. "I'm *not flabby*."

"Sorry, no offense," he tuts. "I meant mentally flabby. You need some fresh air."

"Hugo. If you are going to use your powers of communication and wit purely to insult me, you can just go outside by yourself."

"Great." He's getting very worked up. He takes steps toward me, then steps back, then toward me again, proving it does not, in fact, take two to tango. "I will. Just, you have to come with me. Then I'll stop talking about you being woefully out of shape. And we can play tennis. Let's go."

This is not right. This is not right at all. It's like that thing where animals seem to know that a storm is coming or a meteor or something and they go all loopy before humans know what's coming, but they can't tell anybody, so humans just think they're loopy.

Ah, but we are different, are we not? Hugo and I have the missing power to sort it out.

"What is it, boy? What's wrong?"

"*Boy?* First I'm *Buddy*, now I'm *Boy?* I know it's been two months, but *I* didn't forget *your* name."

"Hugo, come on, what's wrong?"

He gets uncommonly Hugo-serious on me, walking up and butting my leg like a friendly ram. "I don't know. But let's go."

We do go, out of the room and down the hall and out the door and . . .

Holy smokes. Air. Air is such an excellent thing. Wait, the air is doing something. It's moving. It's moving in my direction, into me, up and over my face. Jeez, a breeze.

"What are you doing?" Hugo doesn't approve at all. "Put your arms down, please, before somebody sees us."

I now see that I have been doing the very joyful yet embarrassing childlike maneuver where you hold your arms straight out to the sides like airplane wings. Right on the sidewalk.

"I am an airplane," I say, my arms right up there in full flight.

"You are an airplane with no dog," my dog says, showing me his stumpy little tail and walking away.

"Outside is just so excellent," I say, catching up.

"Yeah, outside's swell. It's one of the best of all possible sides."

"Okay now, what's our plan? Where are we off to?"

"What plan? Who says there's a plan? Zane, you just got out of solitary. Don't you think a nice little cooling-off period is in order, where you just blend back in to society for a while like a nice boy? Isn't that in all our best interests?"

The last thing I want is to blend in to anything. "I feel the exact opposite," I tell Hugo. "I feel like I can't wait to get back into the battle. Dr. Gristle's whole business sizzles with evil, and so far we are the only ones in a position to give him a decent fight. I, for one, want to give it to him, even if you are too chicken."

Even if he is chicken, the reality is that it is scarier to do nothing than to let the not-so-good doctor proceed with his nuttiness unopposed. The whole reason I got locked up in the first place was that I found out how Gristle's work with animals was less about caring for them than it was about programming them and warping them. He made a beautiful blue racing dog run so fast he outran his own life. He shot so many different microchips under the skin of so many different creatures that the military was starting to look at them as one great, giant biological weapon.

And so, Hugo and I got in the way. Anyone with an actual soul would have done the same thing.

We are at the park now and, as usual, we are the only ones at the park. Even the dog walkers have become scarce because, as we now see, the sports center has added a new feature. Not only are there screens inside showing the outside greenery to the people inside, there are also now screens on the outside showing the scenes of activity on the inside to people on the outside. The idea being, apparently, that once you see how fun it is in there, you'll feel like a nert if you're on the outside. And the latest attraction there seems to have tipped the balance greatly. It's a huge indoor walking track/two-lane treadmill for people exercising with their dogs, and it runs the perimeter of the whole games hall. There's a low fence like a long hurdle separating the canine runner from the human one. The critical feature of the dog track is a squeegee-sprayer device that constantly scrapes and cleans the track surface of any dog debris that accumulates, requiring nothing more than a small hop of the dog, and no effort at all from the human, to leave everybody sanitary, happy, and sterile.

Why is nature always the enemy?

Hugo and I stand staring in awe at what we are seeing in there, our faces pressed up close to the screen.

"Makes me want to drop one right here," he says.

"Me, too," I say.

He turns to me. "You're having more trouble reintegrating into society than I had anticipated. Maybe you should go back to being an airplane."

"I am extremely happy to be out. I didn't realize how much I missed —"

"C'mon," he says anxiously, suddenly. "C'mon, c'mon, c'mon, let's go, we have to go, let's get going."

"Going where?" I ask, chasing after him as he takes off even faster this time, straight across the pristine, deserted, never-used, for-decorative-purposes-only soccer field. The mocker field.

"I don't know," he says. "Hurry."

I hurry, of course, chasing after my dog, who says he doesn't know where he is going and yet is commanding me to get there with him, quick.

I follow and follow and follow.

And then I see where he's led me, and the sick feeling in my stomach reminds me why one's dog isn't supposed to make the decisions.

SO, WE MEET AGAIN

"Hugo?" I ask as we stand in the evil doorway of Dr. Gristle's evil veterinary practice. "Hugo, my good friend, why are we here? Did you want to surprise me by taking me straight from prison to the one place that would make me look back fondly at prison?"

"Zane," he says sadly, a little scared, "I swear I have no idea why I came here."

"Ah, puke," I say. "This can't be good."

Just then the big glass door swings open and we are assaulted with the big glass smile of the big bad doctor.

"Boys, there you are," Gristle says brightly. "I was starting to worry. Zane, Zane, Zane." He comes over to me, right there on the top step, in view of the mainly nonevil world, and hugs me more than both my parents ever have.

Ladies and gentlemen, my nemesis.

When he finally lets go and pushes back for a good look-see, he is teary.

"I am so happy you are out. I've missed you. Come in, come in."

I would be less stunned at the greeting if he had opened his mouth and fire came out.

He leads the way back into his establishment. I scoop up my dog and whisper to him, "Insanity alert."

"I told you this from the beginning. The guy's so nuts he sprays his hair with squirrel repellent."

"Why did you bring me here, Hugo?"

"I told you, I don't know why I brought you here. That's the scary part."

"Oh, I think there are lots of scary parts."

We walk down the short, wide corridor, past closed doors and muffled animal complaints. The place is sterile and cold, but not like a vet's building, more like a car wash with plastic palm plants dotted around to make you think it was something else.

"I suppose you are wondering why I brought you here?" says Dr. Gristle as he takes his seat behind the desk in his office. It's a surprisingly cramped office for a powerful wicked scientist. When he folds his hands and leans across his desk, we become far too intimate with his breakfast menu. He is not a vegetarian. Or a flosser.

"I wasn't aware that you had brought us here," I say. "I thought we came here on our own."

The fact that I might not have noticed his neat trick really irritates him.

"Oh, don't be stupid," he snaps. "Why would you do that?"

"Good point," I say, squinting into the fog of pickled pigs' feet, herring, onions, and blue cheese he's just puffed our way. Points for thoroughness — even his breath is sinister.

Brawrf. Hugo coughs.

"Would you like a cookie?" Dr. Gristle asks, his smile returning electric as he rummages around in a desk drawer. "Eureka," he says, and slaps two cookies on the desk.

They are bone-shaped.

"Don't mind if I do," says Hugo. Of course, I'm the only one who can understand him. Gristle isn't wearing a Gizzard™.

Don't mind if I don't, I think — unnecessarily, since they are both already in Hugo's digestive system.

I realize I ran out on my breakfast. I'm the only one in the room who hasn't eaten. This disadvantage could come back to bite me.

"Now, Zane, I realize we have had our differences in the past," Gristle says as he munches on a bone cookie.

"Oh, I thought those were dog treats," I say. "I will take one, if you don't mind."

He cheerfully produces another, and I cheerfully bite.

It tastes like pork fat and mackerel skin–flavored chalk.

"These *are* dog treats," I say.

He waves half a stumpy bone at me. "Keeps both the mind and the teeth sharp," he says.

Fine, can't fall behind. I eat.

"But, my young friend, I see nothing in our colorful past that says we cannot be friends."

"You threw me in jail."

"You have a lovely home. Any boy would be pleased to be thrown there. I'd rather enjoy a spell there myself."

"No!" is Hugo's opinion, and I know we are sharing an image of the doctor coming to stay with us for a visit, like some kind of lunatic uncle who's going to eat the goldfish and grin inappropriately and practice magic tricks until somebody gets horribly maimed.

"No!"

"Hey, don't be nasty. I'm trying to be nice to you."

"Why?"

"Because now with you back prowling the free-world landscape, I think it behooves us to be supportive, rather than destructive, regarding our mutual animal kingdom interests. It behooves us. It behooves the peaceable kingdom. It behooves all earthkind."

"What's *behooves*?" Hugo wants to know. "Is he going to turn everybody into those half-goat things now? If that's it, let's be left out of the behoovering."

I can't suppress a little laugh. Truth is, I don't even try. "Jeez, Doctor, you make us sound all insanely important."

He turns the creepy dial up to eleven now by reaching and grabbing both of my hands before I can react.

"That's exactly how important we are, Zane. *Insanely.*"

Hugo is something like impressed. "Whoa. He makes a compelling case for insanity there."

My mouth hangs open, but nothing comes out. My hands go cold as Gristle squeezes the blood out of them.

"Which is why," he continues, "I can't have you buzzing about like some malevolent hummingbird trying to suck all the nectar out of my genius."

I am trying to free my hands. It isn't working. "Jeez, is that what I was doing?"

"That is precisely what you were doing."

"Heh. Hummingbird." Hugo laughs.

"Sorry about that, Doctor."

"Well, now is your opportunity to make amends, to myself, and to the world. You see this technology I have been employing in handsome Hugo here . . . ?"

Hugo's mind suddenly becomes more open. "Okay, crazy maybe, but certainly not blind."

"You've witnessed the technology that allowed me to guide his movement and behavior to get him to come to me and bring you following."

"Oh, right," says Hugo. "*That's* why we're here. My bad."

"Well, Zane, Hugo is a mere finger puppet in the theater of animal enhancement."

"Speaking of fingers," Hugo says to me, "I really have to remember to stop myself from not biting off his fingers. Let's see how clever he is with stump puppets."

I wish I could laugh. But I know that when Gristle has a plan, it's bad for everyone. Especially me. The cold in my hands runs up my arms and into my whole skeletal structure. His grin and eye-sparks make me afraid to ask him to let go of my hands just as they make me desperate to ask him to let go of my hands.

"So you're talking about bigger stuff," I say.

"I *am* talking about bigger stuff." He leans even closer, smiles even spookier. That's enough for me.

"Could you let go of my hands, please?"

He lets go of the hands, but holds on to the mania.

"The new world starts here, gentlemen."

And with that, there is a knock at the office door behind me. Behind and below, from the sound of it. Sounds more like a tap than a knock, like somebody's hitting a pencil tip against the wood.

"Could you get that for me?" Gristle asks.

I cautiously get up and go to the door. I open it slowly, expecting some kind of trap or another.

Instead, it's a bird.

"Doctor," I say, "there's a bird at the door."

The bird walks right past me, hops up on my chair, then up onto the desktop. He turns around to face me, motionless, like the statue of a falcon. Only smaller, and pale gray.

"Please, sit back down, Zane," the bird says. It's not like with Hugo, with my Gizzard™ translating for me. No, this bird is actually talking out loud.

"How does he know me?" I demand, taking my seat again.

Dr. Gristle is practically giggling with excitement. "He doesn't. He doesn't know you. He doesn't know what he's saying. That's the beauty of the situation! He's a classic bird-brain. He doesn't have to think. He just makes the sounds I create for him. He's like a transmitter for me and my brilliance. Beautiful, no?"

"A unique definition of beauty our pal's got there," says Hugo.

"Um . . ."

"Doc's a genius," says the bird. "He's a great man. Handsome, too. Nobel Prize! Nobel Prize!"

"Well, he was bound to develop some insights of his own. . . ." the doctor modestly adds.

"Doctor, why are you showing me this . . . show?"

"Because, in honor of your release, and our new working relationship for the betterment of myself and every-body, I want you to have him, as a gift and a symbol of my trust."

I have learned that when someone gives you a surpris-ing present, and especially when that someone has recently imprisoned you for thwarting his grand personal awfulness, it is a good idea to take a look at the circumstances. Should the phrase "new working relationship" sound troubling to me?

I stare at the bird more closely now. "You want me to have him?"

"I do. Call it a getting-out present."

I have no desire to take anything from Gristle. It can only bring me trouble. Our old working relationship was, um, imperfect, and I'm not sure how much good it will do to call it "new."

But then something strange happens. It's like the bird changes right before my eyes. He was a thing, a machine, a talking feathered paperweight on a desk, but now I see in his face, a face. He looks at me, and I see somebody in there. It becomes, right now, not about me and the doctor. It's about me and the bird.

It's almost like he needs my help.

I have a sense that he's been trapped by Gristle. Which is something I totally relate to.

"I would have preferred a not-putting-me-in-in-the-first-place present," I mumble. I look the bird in the eye again and feel it begging me to be its escape route. "But . . . okay."

Hugo's still skeptical. "It's a bomb," he insists. "Don't touch it. It's poison. It's got plague."

"What's his name?" I ask.

"Alpha," Gristle says.

"Alpha? That's a bit lab-ratty, isn't it? He doesn't look like an Alpha."

"He is Alpha," Gristle repeats. "He is the starting point."

"I am Alpha," the bird parrots. Though I must say he does it with no enthusiasm at all.

"When does he become mine, like, officially?" I ask.

"Right now."

"Great." I lean closer to the bird and gently poke a finger into his soft puffed chest. "Your name is Alfalfa."

"What?" Dr. Gristle bristles. "That's a *frivolous* name. He's much more important than —"

"Alfalfa," the bird repeats, the feathers on top of his head standing up happily.

The doctor is aghast. "I didn't tell him to say that. That's not at all —"

I have Alfalfa under my arm like a football, and Hugo on the ground running beside me. I open the door, poised for flight.

"Thank you for the gift," I call.

"Thank you," Alfalfa calls.

"I didn't tell him to say that! He doesn't know how to be polite. That bird should not be thanking me."

"I guess I'm a good influence," I say.

"Zane?" Doc asks warmly. Too warmly.

"Yes?"

"In our new spirit of giving, would you perhaps like to share with me your secret? Of your uncanny *rapport* with the animals?"

I smile at him. He smiles at me. As I can only see one of those smiles, I'm going to have to guess that mine is the less frightening.

"The animals asked me not to tell," I say mischievously, while my knees tremble.

"I bet they did," he says right through that smile. "We'll talk," he adds chillingly.

I run.

Once we are a safe distance down the street, I slow down and untuck Alfalfa.

"How are you supposed to carry a bird?" I ask Hugo.

"Do I look like I've carried a lot of birds in my life?"

"Well, no, I suppose not. But you are my go-to guy on these matters. You know animals, generally, better than I do."

"You could let me sit on your forearm," Alfafa instructs. "Or on your shoulder, if you're feeling piratey."

I stop right there on the sidewalk, place Alfalfa on my forearm, and peer into his tiny shiny eyes.

"How can you talk so well?" I ask. I've heard birds who knew a phrase or two before. But this is something completely different.

"Before the doctor did what he did to me, I could just basically imitate sirens and chain saws and ask for crackers.

Now, sometimes I can't sleep from thinking and talking to myself. It's as if now I've got the words so I have to use them. Kind of a mixed blessing. I'm not a birdbrain," he says firmly. "I mean, I am, but the brain of the bird is not what that man implied it is. He's a difficult creature and I am very glad you've liberated me."

This is a very different experience from my previous animal communications. Because Alfalfa doesn't just speak on a screen or through my ear noodle. He is speaking right out loud where anybody can hear him. It is, again, a new level of interaction, one up on the progress we have made up till now, and I have to admit the doctor appears to be pushing the technology forward at an impressive, possibly alarming, rate.

I shouldn't even call them animals anymore. They are Beings.

"So," I say as we walk along toward home, "that was all an act back at the office, with you saying what the doctor wanted you to?"

"Not at all. When he wants to put something in my head, it gets in there, then it comes out of my beak. The acting part was when I pretended I didn't have thoughts of my own. I have plenty of them, but I didn't think it was a good idea to share them with him."

"The only thing you'd want to share with him is bites and bird flu," Hugo adds.

"I would if I could. The fact is, I don't know what I can

do. So much of the time I am doing and saying things that I don't feel, I'm really not very much me at all."

This is not a happy bird.

"I'm happy to be with you guys, though. This is nice."

Maybe for him. But for me, it feels like the beginning of yet another battle with Dr. Gristle.

CAT SLAP FEVER

I'm flying. By that I don't mean I'm in a really good mood or I've had too much coffee or anything else other than *I am flying*. I've left the ground and joined the air and I get it now, I *get* it about flying, as mankind has wanted to get it throughout all of history. Alfalfa is right beside me and he's coaching me and guiding me as we sail at the level of the highest branches of the highest trees in the region, and this is why I get it, because of this final, perfect meeting of the human and animal mind, me and Alfalfa, and my gift, my power, my secret is now bearing fruit like never before, and where oh where oh where can we go from here? I am going to wind up with all the powers of all the great Beings of the planet, and every last person on earth is going to envy me and I am going to enjoy that.

"Cool, no?" Alfalfa says to me.

"Cool, yes. Cool, very, very, yes!"

He drifts in front of me, then beneath me. I bank left and he follows, just like fighter pilots. I don't even have to flap like Alf has to. I merely wiggle my fingers to control my movements. I have it even better than the birds do — it comes so much easier to me than to them, the poor things. I should probably feel a little guilty over my obscene great fortune, but I don't feel anything like that coming on.

"Next, I'm going to get a fish to teach me how to breathe underwater!" I say to my feathery mentor. The sky, and the ocean floor, are now the limit.

"That'll work," he says. "We are all too happy to give you the secrets, Zane."

"That's awfully nice of you guys," I say. "What can I do to repay you?"

"Well," he says, pondering and doing a neat triple barrel roll at the same time. "Say, here's something. Why don't you tell me *your* secret?"

"My secret?"

I'm crashing. I wiggle my fingers like turbo millipedes in a desperate effort to maintain flight, but flight has fled, and the ground is rushing toward me at much greater than head-exploding speed.

"Alfalfa!" I shout. Just before I splat the ground.

My pillow is covered in sweat. My face is pressed deep into the pillow, and the pillow is disgusting.

I was dreaming. I was not flying, which is really disappointing. But I am not splotched on the pavement, which is some consolation.

"Zane, Zane, do you read me?"

I roll over, sit up.

"Of course I read you, Alfie — you're right in front of me."

Alfalfa is sitting on top of the chunky monitor of my old computer. For a second he looks like he, too, is just emerging from sleep, but now he is alert and agitated and speaking in a voice a couple of degrees more sinister and electronic than his real voice.

"Don't call me Alfie. I am Alpha."

Birds probably have facial expressions of some kind. They probably have tics and mannerisms that you could recognize if you were a natural bird, but I am not one. However, I do recognize a difference in Alfalfa when he is talking for the doctor rather than for himself, and it's creepy. He turns into a bird version of a zombie, his body and his head less lifelike, a smokier darkness coming over his feathers and eyes. And he leaves his beak open in an unsettling way even after he's said what he's being made to say.

I look down at the keyboard as I type.

"I'm doing homework right now, Doctor," I say.

"Please don't call me Doctor," the bird says.

I look up and he is back, Alfalfa as himself.

"What's going on, Alf?" I ask.

"I don't know," he says, sounding a little depressed.

"You were just talking to me."

"I know. I sounded like a creep. Sorry."

"So, what — is he gone now? What's he up to?"

Alfalfa does an awkward little move with his wing bones — up, down, but still hugging his sides.

"Was that a shrug?"

"Yes."

"Gotcha."

I love him. He's been here only a week, but I really love this bird. There is something about him, something smart and soulful and deep, and he has already become like some combination of a brother/best friend/confidant. But not at all like a pet.

Hugo is jealous. He doesn't say so, but it's there. He does things like pretending not to be able to understand when Alfalfa talks, and telling inappropriate bird jokes when he knows very well Alfalfa can hear. It's not that I don't understand. Hugo's never had a ton of competition; he's always been top dog, if I may say so. And he *is* still top dog, so he does not have to worry about that.

The thing is, Alfalfa feels like he's more than dog. I can talk to Hugo, and that changes everything, but there is something about Alfalfa that's different, even though he is still a bird and no better or worse than Hugo.

Not better or worse, but more. Alfalfa somehow is more human than Hugo is. Not smarter, but more human.

And Hugo senses this. Or, at least, he senses that I feel this way.

It's a situation I figure will just work itself out, however, and we will all be just —

My thoughts are interrupted by the arrival of another pet. And it's not Hugo.

"Alf—!" I warn.

But I'm too late.

I leap out of my desk chair, but not nearly quick enough. Just like that, Alf is off his perch at the top of my monitor, and I watch in slow motion as he squawks and squeals, flails and falls, nasty to the floor. Sunflower, my cat, takes the whole ride with him, only from the more comfortable position of riding the bird's back. By the time they reach the floor, it's a compressed hurricane of fur and feathers, flashing teeth and snapping beak, screaming, screeching, and blood.

"Sunflower, no!" I shout, throwing myself at them. By the time I reach them, the cat has got a firm grip on the bird's wing, up near the shoulder, and is pulling and twisting so violently he's certain to separate Alfalfa and the wing within seconds.

"Sunflower!" I shout once more, and when he ignores me once more I escalate. I give him such an open hand smack right across his head, he sails into the wall. My hand stings electric.

The cat shoots away and out the open door. If he comes back in again, I swear I will choke him.

I am holding Alfalfa close to me, feeling his heart helicopter in my hands as he tries to break away, bleeding all over me.

"What is *wrong* with that cat?" I shout. "Stupid, stupid animal."

"Nothing's wrong with him," Hugo says. I only now notice he is sitting there, has been sitting there, calm and comfortable, on my bed. "He is a cat. He is doing what a cat does."

Alfalfa is calming in my hands — he might be going into shock.

"No," I say, because isn't that what you say to something like this? "No. Not now. Things are different, here, now. I thought . . ."

"What did you think? Because you could talk to us, you could change us?"

"Well . . . yeah."

"Well . . . no. How could you let yourself believe cats would stop being cats, because you tell them to? Cats are jerks. Cats were jerks before. Cats will continue to be jerks. Cats have the jerk gene and you cannot do anything about that. You need to get something straight, kid: Just because you can commune with creatures, it doesn't mean they're going to stop being the creatures they are. And if that's what you want, then Gristle is right — you *are* on the same side."

I don't have to think twice about the right thing to do now. I stomp over to my bed, take my free hand, and smack Hugo a good hard pop right across his snout.

His great, lovable, magnificent little snowy snout.

He doesn't even blink.

I already feel like punching my own snout, but I have no time for that now. I rush to the door, to head for help for Alfalfa.

Hugo's words accompany me. "You'd better decide what you're in this for, Zane."

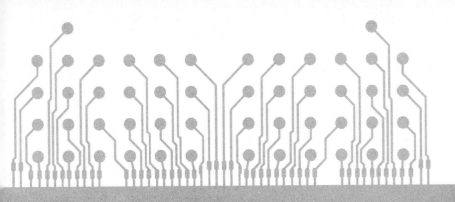

WIP™ 'EM GOOD

I hate to admit it, but there's only one place I can turn. Alfalfa needs medical attention — fast. And there's only one vet nearby. I have no choice but to see Dr. Gristle again.

He doesn't seem surprised to see me — although he does seem surprised to see the state Alfalfa is in. Sunflower really got his claws into the bird.

"Bring me that cat," Dr. Gristle says as he stitches Alfalfa's neck. He has sedated the bird, and is next going to splint the savaged wing. He tells me it's not broken, but it is bent. "I want that cat."

At this moment, I see the doctor as a healer, as a teammate, as somebody who actually does share with me an appreciation for the Beings. Maybe it's just watching him in action, fixing my frighteningly mangled friend. He is very good at his job.

But it also feels like more. Like he is doing more and I am seeing and feeling more than just the application of sutures and antiseptic and bone-mending gentle care. Like I can see beyond and beneath the physical stuff.

I might have been wrong about Dr. Gristle after all.

"I can handle Sunflower, doctor. There's no need —"

"Bring me the cat," he says. "I am going to give him a little something to curb his appetite for winged meat. It's in everybody's best interest."

"Especially mine," says Alfalfa, still lying semiconscious on the table.

Dr. Gristle gives the patient a very funny look.

"He's getting smarter," the doctor says.

"I know," I say. "He is so great."

"Hmmm," the doctor says. "I'll need to follow up with this, and maybe monitor him for a while."

Lying in bed later that night, I watch Alfalfa for signs of weakness. He's fond of perching on the curtain rod above the window by my bed, but it's a tall order for him to get up there just now. So he has taken up residence on the foot-board, and he looks comfortable enough there. It's a good place for me to keep an eye on him, although as I drift off he's giving me a pretty strong eyeball as well. That's kind of weird.

He should be safe, since the room is closed up tight. Even though I haven't been able to locate the cat anywhere since the attack.

"G'night, Alfie boy," I say as my eyes pull closed.

"*Hnnn.*"

I've forgotten all about Hugo, sleeping all the way over in my bathroom, to punish me.

"I said I was sorry, Hugo."

Nothing.

"I said I was sorry. I know you should be sleeping in here."

"*Hnnn.*"

"We'll talk in the morning."

But it feels like we talk all night.

I don't rest very well. I dream. In my dreams I'm looking for the cat. I'm looking everywhere. I can't see him, but I get the unmistakable feeling he is watching me the whole time I'm searching.

The doctor is really not so bad. I misjudged him. I nearly derailed some of the most important joint manimal scientific advancements since Darwin hooked up with the iguanas. I must really try harder. I must do better.

I love Alfalfa. He's a great friend.

I wish Hugo weren't mad at me. No! Hugo is mean. He doesn't even care about Alfalfa nearly getting killed. He's in league with the cat. And he smells. He really should be sleeping in the bathroom permanently. Better yet, he should not be allowed into the room, at least at night. He really does stink.

I love Alfalfa.

Dr. Gristle is a great man. Dr. Gristle is a genius, and I should help support his work in any way that I can. We must get him that Nobel Prize. We must all work toward Dr. Gristle's goals.

I jump up out of bed.

My room bleeps alive, lighting up, ringing, blinking, whistling into action.

"Jeez, what are you doing there, Alfalfa?" I ask, panting.

He is lying on my pillow. The tip of his beak was an inch from my ear. His breathing sounded like whispering.

He sounds all wounded. Probably because he's all wounded.

"I needed to lie down," he says. "I was aching, and getting kind of weak. I'm sorry if I freaked you."

"You didn't freak me," I say, slipping into my slippers as coolly as I can. "I was just dreaming, is all. Don't worry about it, pal."

"Pal," he says, squeak-whistly like a movie pirate-parrot. "Pal, huh? I like it."

With some effort, he flaps his way up to a perch on the headboard. The monitors are all coming on. Newsmama's big handsome head is up high, previewing her show coming on in a few minutes with a "special guest."

"Ah jeez," I say. "It's always the worst when she has a *special guest*. I could interview my underwear drawer and get something more interesting than her *special guests*."

"That's because you have very special underwear," Hugo says, trotting in from his new room. "It has that special scent that brings all *my* friends around."

"Speaking of special scent," I say, "you stink, Hugo. And I mean physically, not just the usual way you stink."

"Special guest," Alfalfa says, in that slightly off voice that gives me a chill. I turn to look at him and he has that hunched, darkened, hardened look again, like he's mounted on top of Edgar Allan Poe's headstone. "Special guest," he repeats. "Special, special guest. Don't miss the specialness."

"Looking kind of scary there, Alf," I say. "Is that you talking for the doc again?"

"Yes," he says lowly, looking at his feet. "I feel cheap as a parakeet after I do that. Please, look away. Don't look at me."

I do him the courtesy of looking away, in time to see my mother's special guest take the seat next to her.

"Oh, I guess she said *mental*, not *special*," offers Hugo.

"He *is* on kind of frequently . . . but so what. Doesn't mean he's not special. Maybe he has something special to show us. He does some very important things, you know, Mr. Cynical Dog."

Mr. Cynical Dog actually rears up on his hind legs and *balances* — and this is *no* circus dog, let me tell you — just to give me his most aggressive off-balance tippy-toe dismissive are-you-kidding-me sneer dance.

"Are you kidding me?"

"Shush."

Up on screen, my Newsmama has already introduced Dr. Gristle, and he is already into his familiar, intense presentation. He leans so assertively in the direction of the home viewers, I almost expect to hear the tink of his forehead hitting my screen.

"And I can promise you that if you join me on my weekly program, which begins this afternoon, you are in for a surprise . . . no, a series of surprises, which will amount to nothing less than the next step in the evolution of life on this planet."

"Wow," I say.

Hugo is less impressed. "Do you suppose he means our planet, or his?"

"I think he means me," says Alfalfa.

"There's a lot of modesty in the air right now," Hugo says. "Has anybody else noticed that?"

"I mean," Alfalfa says, and he does sound modest saying it, "my program. The chip, the technology . . ."

—•—

". . . The interactivity!" the doctor shouts, launching the first episode of his show at three o'clock. "Welcome, welcome, welcome," he says, and I am wondering if the offstage professionals who work on my mother's program are bothering to assist the doctor with his. Because he is clearly too loud. And the set doesn't look at all like a professional tele-visual set. It looks like they are broadcasting from a bad facsimile of his vet practice, with plastic palm trees and cheesy photos of the doctor petrifying celebrity pets. It looks like one of the science classrooms from my school — the old school from before they gutted the place and brought it up to date.

No matter, the doctor fills the screen with his own elec-tricity, enthusiasm, and unique genius.

"And before we go any further, introductions are in order. As long as you and I will be getting to know each other so well in the weeks and years ahead . . ."

"Years?" Hugo can't keep himself from groaning. "Please, Zane, take me for a walk. I have to get something out of my system."

"Shush."

". . . it's only right that you meet my good and trusty right-hand man . . . or, I should say, right-hand simian. Ian, could you come out here please, and meet the people?"

I am riveted to the screen as, after a pause and an angry hand-clap from Dr. Gristle, Ian shyly makes his broadcast debut.

The doctor is beaming, looking right at us.

But he is also alone, as far as we can tell.

After several dull, awkward seconds, the star of the show grasps the whole thing about camera angles and office furniture and stuff, and hauls Ian up onto the desk where the world can admire him.

He looks nervous. Ian, that is. Dr. Gristle looks like he's about to burst out in some Broadway show tunes.

Hugo is unpleasantly curious. "What is that thing?"

"I think it's some kind of monkey," I say.

"It's even uglier than the usual kinds. It looks like a shrunken version of *you* coming out of a bath."

Ian is not, I must say, the most photogenic simian. He's under two feet tall, very thin, a kind of accidental gray, as if his fur has been shampooed in dirty dishwater. He has good posture, though, and good manners, standing at polite attention on the desk.

"Ian," Dr. Gristle says to him, "could you wave to the people, please?"

Ian waves to us. Very cute, the little side-to-side action politicians offer up when they are begging for love.

"Now, Ian, let's do even better. Be cool with the people, Ian."

On cue, little Ian is cool with us. He points at the camera with his right hand, only he makes his hand into a gun shape. He winks one eye and does that cheesy-slick click noise with the side of his tongue.

"Oh, no," I say. "He's invented a sleazeball chip."

"Which I'm sure he calls the SLIP™," Hugo offers.

"Why would he do that, though? His work is so important. He's a visionary."

"Zane, I think you have rabies. Can you get that from a bird? They are filthy, you know."

"I know," Gristle continues, "that you out there are marveling at it all as you watch the lovely Ian here dusting my desk . . ."

He's dusting.

". . . pouring my tea . . ."

He's adding lemon *and* sugar.

". . . and simultaneously humming 'God Bless America' . . . well, sort of . . ."

Not even close — but still, impressive.

". . . You are certainly wondering what kind of miracle we have going on here. Is he a robot? Is this artificial intelligence gone quite literally wild?"

Ian finishes his brief chores, climbs back up on the desk, and straightens the doctor's tie before resuming his Buckingham Palace guard pose.

"It's way beyond robots and AI. That's kids' stuff. What I have developed here involves technology to actually blend the thoughts and wishes of a pet owner with the thoughts and behaviors of the pet owned to such a degree that they function nearly as one organism. Building on the success of my Gristle chip and the Gristle chip 2.0, my patented system is called the WovenIntelligenceProgram, or WIP™. Once a sophisticated beast like my Ian here has been WIP'd™, you have a fully functional, fully biological, superemployee to work with you, amaze your friends, and keep those cocktail parties running smoothly. And before you go wondering whether the monkey is on board with it all, just witness this. Ian, you may love me now."

Ian turns his back to us, his front to Dr. Gristle, and hugs him with the enthusiastic embrace of a tiny little old man clinging to life.

Ian hangs on a bit too long, and the doctor peels him off like the dirty dish towel he resembles.

"So, people, watch this space. Tune in every week as we follow the progress of Ian and his associates as we proceed through the frontiers of scientific discovery. And do send your questions and suggestions to the address on the screen, and either Ian or I will be glad to answer. See you next week."

"Did that monkey just blow a kiss?" Hugo asks.

"Sort of looked like it. He's kind of like the sidekick girl on a game show, huh?"

"Zane, if you let that freak WIP™ me, I'll dig a big hole in the yard to bury myself, and I'll take you with me."

"He's not a freak — he's a genius. It's just a little hard to tell the difference sometimes."

"I'm WIP'd™," Alfalfa says.

"Robot," Hugo sniffs.

"I'm not a robot. I just have a WIP™ chip. I'm still myself some of the time. When the doctor's not bothering me."

"Hugo, don't hurt his feelings. Alf, we know you're not a robot."

No sooner are the words of comfort out of my mouth, than Alfalfa slumps, darkens, and comes out with that creepy alternate voice.

"So, who's next for a WIP™ chip? Did someone say *Hugo*?"

Hugo runs for the door. First he flings himself against it. Then, after bouncing to the floor, just stands there whimpering. It sounds the same in my ear noodle as out in the real air. He has reverted to being pure dog.

Kind of sweet, compared to his lately self.

I know if I talk to Alfalfa when the chip is on, Dr. Gristle will hear me. So I say, "I think Hugo's pretty all set for chips right now, Doctor. It was very impressive, though, I have to say. The televisual presentation. This is amazing work you're doing."

The bird/doctor emits a happy triumphant whistle that indicates Hugo is no longer our focus. "Very glad to see you coming around, young Zane. As I said, you would be a highly valuable contributor to the effort, if you decided to work for the progress of all living creatures, rather than that pointless destructive nonsense you were bent on before."

I wasn't *that* bad.

"I'm ready, Doctor. How can I help?"

"Wonderful. Here's what you can do. Be good. Do your

schoolwork. Get good grades. Get lots of sleep. Stay out of trouble."

Well, then. I certainly feel important.

"Be good?" I say. "Do my schoolwork? You sound like my parents."

"Your parents are wonderful, amazing people, so thank you. The thing is, Zane, you have to get experience and knowledge and judgment before you can be promoted into such big stuff as this. I will be able to tell when you have developed the right approach and attitude for this type of work. And the one thing I've done that your parents haven't is that I have given you a WIP™-powered African gray parrot to manage as an apprenticeship."

"Good point," I say. And just like that, I do feel like an insider, like this is going to get me somewhere.

"So, work with Alpha, watch my program, and get ready for big things."

"Yes, sir," I say. I even salute, which is pretty stupid, but that's how caught up in the possibilities I am.

"Do you see yourself?" Hugo asks. "Something's not right, Zane. You're saluting a bird."

"No, I'm saluting a genius."

"Thanks, I'm flattered, but I am a bird."

Alfalfa has returned to his regular look and sound. So I guess I *was* saluting a bird.

I am startled by my Newsmama popping up on the big screen.

"That's a wordy birdy you have there, Zane. I don't remember giving you that. Did we give you that?"

"Hello, beautiful," Alfalfa says.

"What?" my mother says, startled, then unstartled but still rather pleased. "Oh, well, hello yourself, handsome."

"Love your hair," Alf says, then whistles, then, "Love your show. Never miss it. Never miss it."

He's doing exaggerated cartoon bird, which people seem to like.

"He's amazing," Newsmama says. "You've really been working with him."

"Ah, yes," I say. "You know I'm good with animals."

"You certainly are. Anyway, Dr. Gristle has reminded me that the cat needs to come in for an examination. He has been trying to signal Sunflower's chip, but nothing seems to be happening. It must be inoperable. So you'll need to track him down."

Just then, Alfalfa lets out a piercing, frightened *squawk* in his third language, which is native parrot.

"Oh, there he is now," my mother says. I turn to see Sunflower sitting on the outside of my windowsill, licking his paws and wiping his face.

"Thanks, Mom," I say. "I'll take care of it."

"Right. I'll tell him you will."

She zaps out, and I jump to the window to confront my fluffy little friend.

"All right, killer, where have you been?"

He continues washing his face and hands. I am speaking through glass, but there is no way he can't hear me. And he is chipped the same as Hugo, so there is also no reason he shouldn't be answering.

"Hey," I say, knocking sharply on the glass.

Sunflower pauses and keeps one paw suspended, as if he's going to go right back to it after dealing with the minor annoyance that is me. He opens his mouth, and I can't hear anything.

"What?" I demand.

"Meow," says the cat, slow, drawn-out, bored. "Me. Ow."

That's what he says out loud, out there, on the windowsill, and that's what he says in here, in my ear, through my Gizzard™-translated ear noodle.

I turn angrily to my dog, for a further level of translation. "Do you know what he said to me?"

"Was it, by any chance, 'meow'?"

"Yes. That's exactly what he said. He said 'meow' out loud, and he said 'meow' electronically. What's wrong with him? We have the technology. You can talk, the bird can talk. What's wrong with *him*?"

"I keep telling you what's wrong with him, Zane. He's a CAT. Do you have any idea how stupid you look, standing here trying to talk to a cat? Honestly . . ."

My dog is shaking his whole body in disgust with me. Like he's shaking off after a bath, only it's my stupidity sprinkling all over the room.

"I don't care if he is a cat, he's got the chips in him, he should be talking to me when I talk to him, and he should be receiving when Dr. Gristle's office signals him for an appointment. My room should be announcing right now, that the cat has got an appointment, yet I don't know about you, but *I* don't hear my room speaking. That is the way the world is supposed to work, but what we have here is chaos."

"Calm down. Would you look at your blood pressure up there on the —"

"No, I won't look at it."

"Well, it's just going to get worse. Because the cat isn't going to get better. He hears you, and he hears the doctor's office, and he can respond any time he wants . . ."

I wait. He seems to think I should know how that sentence ends, but he's quite wrong.

"But . . . ?" I ask.

"But, he's a cat," Alfalfa says wearily.

"See, even the bird gets it. Cats got the resistance gene. Always been that way. Always will be that way. They're jerks, too, by the way."

"Great, resistance gene. What good is that to anybody?"

"I sure wouldn't mind having it," says Alfalfa.

I turn back to the window. You know that thing about cats and grins? He lays a fat one on me before casually hopping off the window ledge.

I have been sleeping very funny. One morning when I woke up I was already at my computer, typing away. I must have been there for some time because by the time I realized what I was doing I had accumulated an e-mail about twice the length of one of my school essays. It also made about as much sense as one of my school essays, because I had been happily pinging away at random keys in an effort to set the world gibberish record. And the e-mail was unaddressed.

I'm dreaming a lot. Always, I'm running with the beasts. Or flying or swimming or burrowing with them. I am quite powerful in these dreams, bordering on superhero. When I wake up from these, I still feel amazing. I like this. I would like more of it, in fact.

I think I want to be just like Dr. Gristle when I get older. I want to do important and brilliant work like he does. I want to help him all I can and someday carry on his fine work and become renowned in my own right, but never quite as renowned as he is, just a respectful few rungs lower on the ladder of genius and historical . . .

"Hey!" I shout.

There is a kerfuffle and feathers in the air as Alfalfa awkwardly flaps off to get his just-healing body barely up to his roost on the curtain rod. My room comes alive with light and sound. I am not really even awake yet but I think I'm angry.

Sitting upright in bed, I'm pointing an accusing finger up at the bird. "What were you doing, Alfalfa?"

"What? Me? Nothing. Sleeping."

"Were you on my pillow again?"

"Um . . . that might have been me, I guess."

"Talking? Were you talking to me while I was sleeping?"

"Um . . . it's what I do. You used to like it."

"Were you messing with my mind? Were you brainwashing me, Alfalfa? Is that what's been going on around here? Were you brainwashing me?"

"Um . . . you know, your brain was pretty clean already when I got here."

"Rats!" I shout. I punch my pillow. "Rats and puke and rats."

"Please, Zane, calm down. You're scaring me."

"Good! Wait till I find my cat again. Then you'll know scared."

"Don't do *that*."

"I thought you were my friend."

Hugo's growly laugh is bouncing around the tiles of the bathroom. It sounds like a gathering of the laughing Hugos.

"What's so funny?" I call to him.

"You, ya sap. You're so turned around and upside down at this point, you don't know who's friend and who's foe, do you? People from animals? Fish from fowl? Biology from technology? You don't have a clue, is the truth of the thing, isn't it, Zane?"

I'm still pointing up at the bird accusingly, staring at my dog through my closed bathroom door accusingly.

Until I throw myself back on my pillow, hoping everything will reverse, all my systems and technology will go nice and silent and dim and I can back up into safe and comfy unconsciousness.

"No," I shout instead. "I don't know. I don't know who's what or what's where or anything."

"Of course not, stupid. Why else would you be forcing your man's best friend here to sleep locked up in the bathroom after all these years? That's sure not right thinking."

I bound out of bed and race to the door. "I'm sorry," I say as he saunters out of the bathroom. "I really don't know what I was thinking."

"I believe you were thinking that I stink. Yes, that's what you told me. That's why I had to sleep in the can. My suddenly offensive odor."

"You smell fine," I say, scooping him up and snuffling him like an old favorite teddy bear.

But jeepers, he does not smell fine. Oh, my, he needs a bath.

"Of course I smell fine. I'm as delicious as ever. You only said I smelled because you are a tool. A tool of that bird, who is himself a tool of that quack maniac. There's not a functioning brain here except mine, and I'm embarrassed to be in the same room with you."

Ouch. The only thing to do now is wallow in my shame. When even your dog . . .

"Hey." I interrupt my own wallowing. "You're a tool, too, Hugo. Remember when he made you bring me to his office? And you obeyed like a little toy robot dog?"

He sits down. "Ah, I forgot about that. Fine, we're all losers. We're all tools. Doctor Fathead Vet Jerk wins."

"No. He can't win. We can't just buckle like that. Somebody's got to have the strength not to be a tool."

From the windowsill comes a lazy, "Meow."

"Ahhh," screams Alfalfa, even though the cat would have to be bionic to reach him up on the curtain rod.

"How did you get in here?" I ask Sunflower.

"Meow," says Sunflower.

"I have had just about enough of this from you," I say, walking forward and menacing my cat with my very scary pointer finger.

Hugo is laughing again.

"You, too," I shout at my dog. "This isn't funny. We have to do better than this, all of us, together. . . ."

Alfalfa squawks even louder, and scareder, and I turn yet again to find Sunflower very calmly and carefully climbing the curtain like a marine going up a rope ladder.

The bird is frozen up there, and even crying, like a human baby.

Serves him right, the brainwashing fink.

Ah, puke.

I rush over and tackle Sunflower right down off the curtain. I wrestle him to the floor, and the fight is fairly furious. His claws are everywhere — he has, like, fifty of them, and they're sharp and glinting like knives.

The result of a life lived basically chair-to-bed-to-school-to-chair-to-bed is that it turns out I am almost exactly as strong as my cat, who weighs eleven pounds. Then factor in his reflexes — which are, unsurprisingly, catlike — and, oh, yes, those claws, and —

"Help! Isn't anybody going to help me?" I plead.

Hugo is on his back, rolling side-to-side with helpless and unhelpful laughter. Alfalfa has gathered up all his courage and gratitude over what I'm doing for him, and flown smack into the door in an effort to escape.

I eventually manage to get on top of Sunflower, dragging my bedspread down off the bed and smothering him up like a spitting, snapping sack of vicious laundry.

I am panting as I hold him to the floor.

"We are supposed to be a team," I say to everybody, anybody, nobody.

"Who supposes that?" Hugo asks, collecting himself and coming closer.

"We *should* be a team," Alfalfa says, fluttering over to perch on my computer monitor. "We will need to work together."

"Of course featherboy wants to be on a team. He's parrot parmesan without us to protect him. What does he have to trade?"

"He can fly," I point out. "And he has the power of speech."

Hugo is not happy that I have pointed this out. First he lets something silent and rancid poison our air, then declares, "I could do that stuff if I wanted to."

"Right. What do you say, Sunflower?" I ask the bedspread.

"Meow," it replies, then bursts into a whirl of hissing fury.

"Fine," I say, hanging on like a rodeo rider. "Dr. Gristle keeps telling me he needs to see you, so I guess I might as well just bring you to him, then."

The bedspread stops fighting, calms right down.

"It's a trap," Alfalfa squawks. "Don't let him out. Just pick up the bedspread and beat it against the floor a few times. He's not to be trusted."

"What's the bird talking about?" Hugo says. "He doesn't even know him."

"So you think it's all right?" I ask Hugo.

"Oh, no, he's going to bite the bird's head off first chance he gets. I just don't think the bird has any right to be judging him."

How is this ever going to work?

"How is this ever going to work, guys?" I ask.

"Meow."

It's only a meow, but it's not a helpful meow. It's a deeply cynical meow.

"As far as I'm concerned, I'll do whatever you want," Alfalfa says. "I don't want that doctor living inside my head, and I can bet that monkey doesn't, either."

Hugo is indignant. "Is he implying that I *do* want the doctor living in my head? Does he suppose I am just a happy little tool, not as sophisticated as a hypnotist bird or a house-keeper monkey? I'm willing to do whatever it takes, too."

"Good, good," I say. "This is what we need. Cooperation. Together, we've really got something. Dr. Gristle is a pretty formidable character, but as a team, we can be a fearsome force ourselves. I mean, he is brilliant. A genius. His mind is an awesome and powerful force of nature before which we are individually only puny insignificant . . . *ouch!*"

"That's right," Hugo says, "I bit you. Your brain is still so washed you have suds coming out of your ears. So I bit you, and I will continue to bite you every time you start bub-bling up any more of that ridiculous nonsense."

He's right. I don't seem entirely in control, and it's good to have him covering me.

"Thanks, pal," I say. "Sometimes I forget how good you are for me. You're a true and great friend and if I ever didn't have you by my side . . . *ouch*!"

"You were getting sappy. I will also be biting when you get sappy."

"Fair enough."

"What about the cat?" Alfalfa asks nervously.

"Sunflower," I say, "are you with us in the resistance to Dr. Gristle's brilliant . . . sorry, wicked plans?"

Sunflower's response is not shocking. "Meow."

I turn to Hugo for enlightenment.

"I don't really speak cat, but I think it's fair to say that the cat has decided to run his own resistance. To everything. Best option, I'm afraid, is to stuff him out the window."

"I don't want to be disagreeable," Alfalfa adds, "but I have to support the stuff-him-out-the-window plan."

Under the circumstances, I have to say it is probably the sensible plan. And Sunflower's final "meow" sounds very much like his endorsement of the plan.

Out the window he goes.

But I pause just before I open the window. Sunflower looks anxious and pleased and ready to bolt, but startled when I hesitate and pull him close.

"I know you are following everything," I whisper. "And

obviously you are not the most popular member of the team, but still, to me, you *are* a member of the team."

"Meow."

"Yeah, yeah, I get it. You are the king of resistance. We are going to need that at some point."

He stares at me and hangs there lifelessly, like I'm holding up a very bored baby by the armpits. Eventually he opens up his mouth.

"Meow," I say, beating him to the punch and happily stuffing him out the window.

I am certain, as he spills to the ground, I hear a very faint, sly, "Chump."

"Dr. Gristle knows that cats are the biggest threat to birds. That's why he wants to get Sunflower into his office. Who knows what he'll do to him if he gets his hands on him."

"Let's find out," Hugo says.

"Let's not," I say.

We are heading on a trip to visit our old friends out in the WildWood, and the WildArea beyond, for the first time since I got out of confinement. I have had no contact with them for over two months, so have no idea what to expect. I'm hoping it has become a free and untroubled paradise for creatures who just want to be creatures.

The last I saw, WildWood was cleared of Beings as we helped them all disperse to the WildArea where Gristle and his Gristlie goons couldn't track and trouble them. But I never even saw the WildArea, and can only guess what they found there. The hope was they would be able to at some point filter back into the Wood, at least on a part-time basis. It was their home. It was a wonder of a place, and even the

WildWater at the center of it, so mysterious and dangerous, was something nobody really wanted to get away from.

I'm thinking, as we slip from the wide-open sidewalk into the cool hug of the woods, that many of the Beings would have been unable to wait. I am expecting to find life here.

Hugo has more bounce to his walk than usual. He normally doesn't like to express a great deal of affection for . . . anyone or anything, really. At least not outwardly. But his stout little body can't lie, and he's happy to be hitting the old neighborhood.

"I still don't trust that bird, by the way," Hugo says, straining for something to be disagreeable about.

Somebody needs a little positive reinforcement.

"Who's a pretty boy?" I say, as sickly as sweet can be.

"I am. What's it to you?" comes the slow response, the words pulling out like very cold taffy.

"Goth Sloth?" I say happily, scanning the branches above all around. "You're a sound for sore ears. What's happening? Where is everybody?"

"WildArea. They all thought it was *so* wonderful, *so* magical, *so* perfect. . . ."

"I get it, Sloth. You, I take it, felt otherwise."

"Correct. Being all happy like that is *so* lame. I couldn't stand it anymore."

"Keep fighting the good fight there, GS."

"Speaking of fighting, there is an occupying army here in the WildWood."

It is important to remember that Goth Sloth sees the whole world through dark, hairy glasses of negativity.

"I'm sure there is no army here. Ants, maybe? Are you moaning because some ants have set up nearby?"

"Nobody ever believes me. Nothing even matters. Why do I even try? You don't understand. You don't even care. I should never even have been born. You're just a —"

"Sloth," I cut in, though cutting in on Sloth isn't the hardest thing to do, since there are about twelve seconds of dead air after each word. "Just tell me about this so-called army."

"I'll do better than that. I'll show you."

He is climbing down the tree headfirst. Each claw digs deeply and securely into the bark before he moves the next one into place. His progress is almost imperceptible to the naked eye.

"Why don't you just point me in the direction?" I say.

Goth Sloth seems to think this over for a while. Then he looks at each of his front claws, like he's deciding which is up to the job of pointing.

"Come on," Hugo says, running off, "just follow my nose."

Which I do, sort of. Hugo follows his trusty nose, while I follow his trusty other end, until in just a few seconds we stop short, in a thicket several yards from the bank of the killer WildWater pond. There, we encounter . . .

"An army?" Hugo asks.

It's not an army, of course. It might be even worse.

There are about twenty monkeys, macaques just like the one Dr. Gristle had on his show. Only they are not domestic housekeeper types. They are standing at attention, while one of the doctor's big Gristlie goons barks commands at them.

"Fold your arms!" the Gristlie shouts.

As a group, the entire gang of monkeys assume a casual arms-folded pose, like they are observing a parade or something.

"What kind of a command is that?" Hugo asks.

"Now, smile," Gristlie shouts in such a way that the last thing anyone would want to do is smile. They all smile anyway.

"Now that is creepy," says Hugo.

It certainly is.

We watch as the macaques are run through their paces, acting as human as any two-foot gray simians can. They do little dances, they practice pretending to laugh at unfunny jokes, they even go through something like speech lessons. They never accomplish any words, exactly, but they warp their natural monkey screechiness and chatter into screeches and chats that seem to make as much sense as most people you could talk to.

At one point the drill instructors stop shouting out any commands. The monkeys must still be responding to something, however, because they continue executing crisp maneuvers without the bossing. Mostly what they seem to be enacting is a fair impression of a polite little society.

The overall effect is weirdly relaxing. In very short order, the two rows of ten macaques have evolved, right in front of my eyes. They have gone from slightly frightening, incorrect monkeybots, to a group that could just about pass for a very short and hairy but not unpleasant birthday party. If people were more like this, I might have more of them for friends.

"Just look at them," says Hugo. "Couldn't you just shove every last one of them into the pond?"

"No," I say a little more loudly than I had intended, "I think they're great."

My voice must have traveled. The Gristlie wheels and looks in our direction with eyes that look like bloodballs. She stares, and it is a way uncomfortable stare, even though I don't think she can see us.

More unsettling still, every pair of macaque eyes is also trained our way, and with the identical look, as if their leader somehow controls them, enters them, possesses them. Their cute monkey smiles have long gone, and the birthday party looks more like a hunting party.

I don't even detect a cue, but the macaques start a mini-march, falling into formation double-file, heading directly our way.

"Apparently the party was invitation-only," says Hugo.

"Ants, huh?" comes Sloth's voice halfway up a tree right behind us. "Maybe somebody will finally start believing me."

Then Goth Sloth does something I find remarkable. He moves. A lot.

He begins violently shaking his tree and letting out a kind of grunty-ooky noise that has all the macaques looking up.

"This is the point where you run, genius human," he says to me.

"Thanks," I shout, and bolt back through the woods as the macaques climb and swarm to investigate. It suddenly feels like there are hundreds of them up there.

"Monkeys," Sloth says with disgust. "Just look at them — they all think they're better than me."

Maybe he'll bore them into submission.

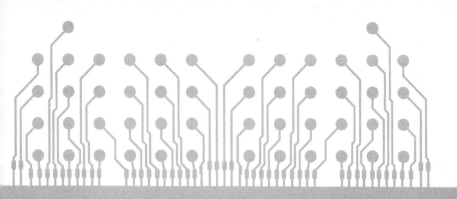

BEAUTIFUL BRUTES

We come home to a surprise. For the first time I can remember, I am greeted at the door.

"Oh, rats," I say when the door swings open.

"I think you mean, *oh, macaques*," says Hugo.

Which is exactly what we have. Like a tiny, dignified doorman, a monkey stands there attentively waiting for us to step inside.

I don't care if he has nice manners. Hugo and I bolt past him, down the hall and into my room. The room lights up, the old sights and sounds kicking in. Then That Voice comes booming out of the ceiling speaker. He's trying to sound cool, but obviously he's been dying for me to run into this.

"So," Dad says, "you've met my personal assistant?"

"Dad, why is he here?"

"Dr. Gristle sent him. His name is Munson and he is one of the very first graduates of the academy. The doctor said we are just the type of family these guys are meant for, so he wanted us to have him."

My Newsmama's big beautiful head pops up on the screen. "Have you met him yet? I mean, don't you love him? How could you not love our Munson?"

"I try not to fall in love that easily," I say.

Sometimes I think the connection isn't very good because my mother seems to hear different answers from the ones I give her.

"I know," she says. "I don't know how we ever managed without one. When the doctor introduced me to him and showed me his capabilities — well, I was overwhelmed, let me tell you. Have you checked his schedule? He's a dynamo. This afternoon he's giving Hugo a bath."

You know when people say they are *beside themselves*? Well, only dogs can come really close to achieving it.

Hugo goes into a fit.

"That *grrr* monkey is *grrr* not *grrrrr* bathing me. . . ." he says, snorting, snapping, and chasing his own tail in a furious circle that eventually makes him look like a little white blur of two demented dogs. I'm not happy Munson is here, but the effect on Hugo is kind of fun.

"What's wrong with him?" Newsmama asks.

"I think he's beside himself."

"Well, pull him together before he gets hurt."

"Maybe Munson can handle it."

"*Grrr.*" Hugo accelerates to the point where he is officially invisible, until he breaks out of his own orbit and crashes into the wall.

There is a knock at the door.

I open it to find Munson there with a bottle of flea shampoo in his hand and a towel over his arm.

"I do not have fleas!" Hugo says, launching himself in the direction of Munson. Fortunately the dog is so dizzy he misses the opening completely and smashes into the door frame.

"Maybe later," I say to Munson, shutting the door for his own safety.

"You are only embarrassing yourself," I say to Hugo.

"Yeah, well, next time I'll try harder, and embarrass *everybody*."

"Listen," That Voice says, "I have got to get back to working. Zane, you need to make sure things run smoothly there. Work Munson into the team. Make Hugo play nice with others. And why is that bird being so quiet?"

"He's mad at me because he's in protective custody."

Alfalfa is in a good strong cage for the time being, to protect him from Sunflower. He doesn't agree with the decision. We had words over it. Now we don't have any words at all.

"Well . . . see what you can do," Dad says, and signs off.

"Yes, Zany," Newsmama says. "See what you can do." And she signs off.

My parents are big fans of that. Of signing off, and of me seeing what I can do. Because they don't really believe I can do all that much.

As disagreeable as Hugo can be, I have to agree with him on this one — I don't trust the monkey. Like with everything Dr. Gristle does, there is something else going on underneath it. So while Munson may be quite capable of vacuuming and making tea, deadheading the rosebushes and screening calls from salespeople, I am not letting him inside our tight group. At least not until I can find out more about what's going on.

I make my one effort to open discussions with him when he comes to my door at bedtime. I answer his knock and find him standing there with a small silver tray and a mug of hot chocolate with a marshmallow island floating on top.

"Oh," I say, suddenly forgetting all of my suspicions because, yes, I can be brainwashed almost instantly by a single marshmallow. I take the mug and try to talk to him.

"You are chipped, right, Munson? You've got the WIP™ chip and all that?"

He stares at me. He does his scary little smile thing. Then he waves. Then he stares some more. Then he shrugs.

"Can you talk to me? You can, right? Do you know who I am? I'm The Friend. Are you okay? What is the story with the simian academy?"

There is a longer pause, and a face straining across Munson's tense features as it looks like six different feelings are struggling to declare themselves on his face.

"Ah, ah, ah, ah adda addas adda ahhh . . ."

It is an unnerving, tortured, shrieky voice — no, voices — in my ear noodle now as Munson tries to talk to me. There are several distinct signals at once, bouncing all around the inside of my head, and I am just about to tear the noodle out of my ear because the sound is excruciating, but then he stops short.

I'm rubbing at my ear, looking at him, and he shrugs meekly.

"How many chips are in there? How much monkeying does it take to make a monkey personal assistant?"

He shrugs. He waves, bows, and walks down the hall. Slouching. Then forcing himself back up straight.

"One cup of cocoa," Hugo says as I shut the door. "You sad, pathetic little man. That's your price? The doctor sends his little henchman, and the henchman brings a cup of cocoa, and, just like that, you are sold."

"I'm not sold," I say. "It's just, he didn't seem so bad, did he? I think he's troubled."

"I think *you* are troubled. And you'd better not let your guard down, Zane, or we will be in jeopardy."

"I'm not letting my guard down," I say. "But I *am* going to bed."

"Sounds like letting your guard down to me."

"Oh, okay, you can stay awake for the rest of your life if you like, but I'm going to sleep."

I walk back to bed, finish my very fine cup of hot

chocolate, and go to Alfalfa's cage. "Don't think of it as a cage," I say. "Think of it as an unusually safe balcony."

"Prison," is all he chooses to say.

"I've been in prison," I tell him. "I understand. This will only be temporary."

I leave him there on the desk, and go to bed.

I am skimming along through the trees. Hand over hand over hand, with all the grace and power the monkey gods could give me. This is almost better than flying because I feel not just light and fast and carefree. I feel all that, but also . . . brutal, in the best possible way. I am a brute. I am a beautiful brute, and every ape in the forest is following me because I have it all, the power and the brainpower, and I could just about explode with the joy and the immensity of who and what I am and what I might be able to do.

You can never have enough of this. I can never have enough of this.

I *love* that I am the king of the beasts.

"What are you *doing* here?" I shout, yet again, at my bird.

"Nothing," he says. "Just sitting on my uncommonly safe balcony, minding my own —"

He is sitting on his balcony. But his balcony is no longer on the desk where I left it. It is on the night table right by my head.

"You were talking to me all night again, weren't you?" I am really bellowing at him now. "I cannot even go to sleep in my own bed without . . . the genius of Dr. Gristle becoming more obvious all the time! I have a good mind to . . . go right down to his office and beg him to let me help with his projects in any way that I can . . . to join forces with him and harness the greatness that is there just for us to —"

Rats. I'm doing it again.

"Rats!" I say. "I'm doing it again! Hey, Alfalfa, how did your cage get from the desk over to my night table? I'm certain I left you all the way over there. . . . Hugo! Hugo, wake up."

Hugo even now only grudgingly wakes up.

"Hugo, did you see what happened? Do you know how Alfalfa's cage got over here in the middle of the night?"

"Sorry, boss, I guess I slept through it. I tried to stay awake for the whole night — I was standing up, right over there, and I was doing well, too . . . then next thing you were screaming for me to wake up. See, told you about letting our guard down."

"I called the monkey," Alfalfa says.

"You what?"

"I called the monkey." His top head feathers are flattened down in shame, as well they should be. "That is, the doctor, through me, called the monkey in, and the monkey brought me over to you."

"Arrggh," I shout, punching my pillow. "This is a nightmare. There is no escaping this. Day and night, lightness and darkness, there is no place to go to avoid . . . the awesome power of Dr. Gristle's intelligence and imagination, which will eventually prove to be the greatest — *ow!*"

"I told you, if you started that stuff again, there would be biting," Hugo says. "And there is plenty more where that came from."

"Thanks," I say.

"This is terrible," Alf says. "I am so ashamed. There you are getting bitten by that mean, ugly little dog because of me. . . ."

"Hey, hey, hey . . ." Hugo protests.

"All because I cannot manage the strength to keep Dr. Gristle from controlling my thoughts."

"Hey," I say, "it isn't your fault. The doctor is a force beyond anything we have seen, and it's — *ouch!* Hugo, try to pay attention. I wasn't saying that was a good thing."

"Sorry. I owe you one. I won't bite you one time when you deserve a bite."

"I don't know why you don't just let me out of this cage and bring on the cat."

"Sounds reasonable," Hugo says. "Shall we take a vote?"

"Stop that," I say. "Nobody is biting anybody's head off. We are all to one degree or another part of Dr. Gristle's modest little experiment at controlling every single living thing on earth. So our only chance is to put our differences aside, work as a unit, and watch each other's backs. Agreed?"

Alfalfa and Hugo eye each other up.

"Hugo's a dolt," Alfalfa says out loud.

"Alfalfa's a weenie," Hugo says in my ear noodle.

"That's the stuff," I say, and leave them to bond while I go have my breakfast.

Breakfast ends up being a different experience from what I am used to.

"Do you have to stare at me?"

Munson won't stop staring at me. He's a starer. I am trying to roll my sausages neatly into my pancakes, but the pancakes are a little too thick for pigs in a blanket, so it's a struggle and I'm already getting frustrated. Munson sees my plight, runs right up, and rolls one with the dexterity of a cigar maker. Then he scurries back to his mark to continue standing at attention and staring at me.

Monkey hands. There have been monkey hands touching my food. Who knows where those hands have been?

"Honestly, do you have to stare at me?"

It's extremely sad. Munson, wishing to please me, but not knowing what to do with himself, looks down at his feet, up at the ceiling, out the window, then at his fingernails. But he stays at attention.

"Tell you what," I say. "Why don't you go down to my room and bring back Hugo. Can you do that?"

He's down the hall before I even finish. I remove the blanketed pig and set it aside on my napkin. In a few seconds the two are back, Munson standing guard and Hugo at my side.

"Yes?" Hugo asks.

"Here, I was feeling generous." I hold the food in front of his nose.

"Does this have monkey hand on it?" Hugo asks. "Because I believe I smell monkey hand."

It is a certain waste of time to try and lie to him on something like this. "Yes," I say.

He swallows it in one bite.

"Call me if you need my skill set again," he says as he toddles back down the hall.

"What are you doing?"

"Bird and I are brainstorming."

"How's that working out?"

"Mostly I nod. He does the bulk of the talking. He's actually very interesting."

Well, what do you know. That's a fine development, and all I had to do was get out of their way. Something to remember there.

"So, Munson, looks like it's me and you for breakfast," I say. "Why don't you tell me a little about yourself." I offer him my banana.

He raises a polite hand and gently waves me off.

"Oh, I do wish you could tell me," I say through a mouthful of food.

Munson puts a finger to his lips and shakes his head at my poor manners.

"Sorry," I say.

By the time I've finished my meal, I am satisfied and relaxed and feeling pretty good about things. Hugo and Alfalfa are getting along so well I haven't heard a thing down there for a half hour. I finally convince Munson to take half a banana, and somehow without words we are getting along, as they say, like a house on fire.

Come to think of it, is that really a good thing, a house on fire?

"Well, guys," I say as Munson and I come swaggering into my bedroom. Or at least I swagger. Munson is a little too formal to swagger, so he just walks. "How is everything going in here?"

"We have to get that cat," Alfalfa says bluntly.

"Yes," Hugo agrees, "we have to get that cat and bring him to Dr. Gristle for readjustment."

"Readjustment," Alfalfa echoes.

"He can't ever be a part of the team," Hugo explains. "The whole point of watching each other's back is that you kind of count on the next guy to watch your back without eventually jumping on it and biting your spine in two."

"It is absolutely the right thing to do," Alfalfa says. "If we are to be a team and get anything done."

"Cats don't play," Hugo says.

"Cats don't play," Alfalfa says.

I turn to my latest associate to see his reaction to all this. His reaction is to be gone already. Off polishing silver or something.

"Well, I guess," I say, walking to the closet to get my jacket.

Just then, the screen on my wall that scans the outside world around the house goes wild. There is a major scrapple going on in the border plants in the backyard, and all of us look up, riveted to the action like it's a big sporting event, only not boring.

Tumbling out of the undergrowth are Sunflower . . . and Munson.

The cat is not that much smaller than the macaque and — as I discovered myself — well-armed with tooth and claw and vicious power. But there is no contest here. Munson is like some kind of commando, on the cat's back and woven all around him, tangling legs together, putting him in a near death grip under the chin. Sunflower is wild with rage, but, by the second, we see him lose strength, steam, and chance. First Munson was hanging on desperately, but now the action is more like a python death grip.

"Come on!" I shout anxiously to the team as I bolt out the door toward the scene.

The team is not nearly so anxious. Alfalfa is excused from following, since he's in a cage and all. But the level of who-cares in that room is still extremely high.

Sunflower is actually unconscious as I approach the tangle. Munson, despite the intensity of the battle, is entirely cooperative, letting go as I reach to collect the cat.

"Go in the house, and close that door behind you," I say. "I'm going to the vet's."

Munson follows instructions to the letter. I am in awe now at what an efficient killing machine/gentleman he is.

Sunflower begins to revive as we approach the doctor's office. I have been carrying him like a baby, cradling him on his back and rubbing his belly and stroking his macaqued throat.

He opens his eyes. He licks his lips several times, lets out a coughlike little noise. He blinks, he blinks, his eyes clear, and he fixes me, recognizes me.

And launches himself right at my face.

"Hey," I shout, "what are you getting at *me* for? It wasn't me who knocked you out, it was the monkey."

Sunflower swipes at my face and hisses at the sound of the word *monkey*. I am holding him at arm's length, still awkwardly making my way toward the office.

"I am trying to help you, jerk cat. You need to see Dr. Gristle."

The doctor's name sends the cat even nuttier than the monkey thing did. He is really thrashing now, clearly back to something like full strength, which is still just about equal to my strength. My arms turn out not to be as long as I thought they were, because Sunflower's right front paw catches me with a punch in the temple, while the rear left neatly snaps my chin.

"Right," I say, pinning him flat to the wall of the vet building. The cat and I are both panting heavily. "You apparently don't wish to go to the doctor's office. I'll make you a deal: You *tell* me why not, and I'll let you leave right now."

Sunflower takes a break from trying to slice up a side of Zane bacon. He looks at me intently, yet calmly.

"I know you can talk to me. I know you are chipped and you can talk to me fine."

He curls a little one-side smile, then speaks. "Mee. Yow."

I have a very strong-willed cat.

"*There* you are!" Dr. Gristle throws open the front door and nearly spooks me and the cat into the street, reducing our combined lives to eight.

"Hello," I say.

"Meow," Sunflower says without his usual self-confidence. He even speeds it up a bit. "Meow-meow-meow-meow."

We follow the doctor in, and I can't help but pressure the cat. "Sorry, Sunflower, would you care to elaborate on that? I couldn't quite —"

He elaborates by raking an excellent swipe across my forehead and nose.

When we are seated in the examining room, it is hard to tell who is the patient. I am sitting on the exam table with Sunflower pressed to my chest in a bear hug.

"I was starting to wonder where you were," Gristle says, smiling broadly and touching my face scratches with his finger. "I expected you a while ago."

"Well, we would have been here sooner, but I was busy losing a street fight to my cat. . . . Hey, what do you mean you expected us? I didn't tell you we were coming."

"I know," he says, all excited, like I am unwrapping an amazing gift, but taking way too long doing it. "It's all going so well, it's hard to keep up. Well, it's not hard for me, because I'm doing it all, but for you . . ."

He is now swabbing my scrapes with something that burns and therefore must be good for me.

"Yes, for me it's confusing, so could you fill me in?"

He's giggling. He can't explain to me, because he is giggling. I feel the hair stand up all over the cat. The few hairy places I have do the same thing. It's a lot less fun than it sounds.

"Doctor?"

"Yes, yes, it's just all so thrilling. It's the bird, Zane. The bird — he convinced you, yes, that the cat had to come to me."

"Well . . . yes, I suppose . . ."

He's giggling again.

"Doctor, Sunflower is trembling. Could you maybe stop that laughing?"

"But this is wondrous. The third-party communications system is evolving more quickly and smoothly than I had anticipated. I have been able to communicate my wishes through the bird, resulting in you bringing the cat to me."

"Right. I think I follow now. And having the monkey attempt to assassinate the cat was a way of making sure I had reason to bring the cat in."

"Pardon?"

"The monkey. The macaque. You got the bird to tell the monkey to attempt to kill the cat, and that's why we are all here right now. I mean, pretty ingenious, I suppose. But an e-mail might have worked just as well."

Gristle pulls back from me, his face goes scarlet, accentuated by his standy-uppy blond hair, dazzling teeth, and pale, prime-time eyes.

"No, no, no!" he insists. "The monkey was not supposed to kill the cat. The monkey was not supposed to kill the cat, and the bird was not supposed to tell the monkey to kill the cat. What is *wrong* with everybody?"

"Like I said, maybe just send a message next time. . . ."

"I have to talk to that bird, for one thing, that's for sure. And what is that monkey doing taking orders from the bird?"

"Yes," I say. "About that? That does seem to be an unusually charismatic bird. I think if he could run for public office, he would get about one hundred percent of the votes."

"Meow," says Sunflower.

"Right, just under one hundred percent. Sunflower can't stand him. What exactly is it about this bird —"

"Right," Dr. Gristle interrupts, switching gears very quickly to sweet neighborhood veterinarian. He reaches toward the cat, attempting a belly stroke. In response, Sunflower goes rigid as a scratching post. "Look at our friend Sunflower here. Still attempting to disembowel Alpha, is he?"

"Alfalfa, you mean. And yes, that does still seem to be on Sunflower's mind. Though he's more interested in the back of the neck than the bowel."

"*Back* of the neck?" This detail seems to grip the doc. He peers right into Sunflower's yellow eyes. "Right. Can't have you damaging any sensitive biotechnology there, can we? No, no, we cannot have that." He steps back, strokes his chin, smiles unconvincingly. "We can fix that little problem, I think. Just you two wait right here."

When the doctor is out of the room, Sunflower immediately does the oddest thing I have ever seen him do. He turns his head. All the way around, like I hear owls can do though I have never actually seen it myself. He is nose-to-nose with me, and his eyes are also big as an owl's.

Sunflower is uncommonly scared. And his expression is telling me more, and telling me more clearly than he ever would even if I could get a million words out of him.

"Easy," I say, trying to reassure him with all the wrong words. "What are you giving me that look for? I'm scared stiff, and I'm not even the one getting whatever the doctor is bringing."

If you didn't know better, you would think I was holding a taxidermied cat.

I hear the doctor's footsteps.

"Are you going to stop killing Alfalfa?" I ask.

Nothing.

"Come on, Sun, work with me here."

This is a tough cat, and I am growing in admiration by the second. I still want to smack his whole petrified self off the edge of the table, but I am growing in admiration.

I walk him over to the window. I don't open it yet.

"I don't want him to hurt you, Sunflower. Talk to me."

"Meow."

"Cripes. Talk to me."

The doctor's stopped outside the door by a nurse asking if she is really supposed to be taking orders from the nasty cockatoo sitting at the desk in his office. It turns out she is. His hand is on the door.

"Are you going to talk to me?" I growl at my cat.

He snarls, which can look cute when a cat does it with his little lippage — but no, this isn't cute.

"No," he says.

"Good enough for me," I say, and shove him right out the window into the fresh cool air. I hear cars screeching to a stop and wonder which life he's on, anyway.

"Oh, Zane," Dr. Gristle says, shaking his head sadly. He is holding either a large needle or a small harpoon. I'm going with harpoon, because it's also got wires trailing off the back of it. "We were making such progress, we were."

I debrief later with Hugo.

"Well, you're here, so at least he didn't kill you."

"No, Hugo, he didn't kill me. He didn't do a lot of anything, actually. He said he had to go to the studio and do his show, and he wanted me to go home and think about what I had done."

"Think about what you've done? That's a pretty lame punishment. Last time you got jailed for two months! I have to say, you're really plummeting into insignificance."

"Maybe I'm still significant, wise guy, and the doctor is just a nicer guy than you thought."

"That's a good point," Alfalfa adds. "Doc has his good points. And he wants to be your friend."

"You think?"

"I think."

"I think, too. But I think other things than what you think," Hugo says.

"Like what?"

"Like I think none of us know what's up with the doc, least of all you."

"I think you're right," I say. I think I need to sleep or my head is going to explode. "Hugo, I want you to lie right here next to my bed, and don't leave all night. Alfalfa, go to sleep, and don't say anything until tomorrow morning. I am going to sleep on this, and if nobody messes with my brain between now and breakfast, I'll have a clearer sense of everything. Right?"

"Right," Alfalfa says enthusiastically.

Hugo doesn't say anything.

Instead, he snores.

I don't know where I am. I'm not exactly in the middle of nowhere, but I'm certainly on the outer edges of it. I may even be underwater, for all the murky, peaceful, unclear smoothness washing over my face and my eyes and my brain. I have never felt so calm and sure in my life, even if I have no idea what it is I am sure of.

I wake up sitting across the desk from Dr. Gristle, his unreasonably brilliant smile the thing that has most likely woken me. We are shaking hands.

"I think we will both be happy that you made this decision, Zane."

Shake shake shake.

"I think we will be, too," I say.

Shake shake shake.

I do not know what decision I have made.

"You will enjoy working here, learning both the every-day veterinary business and the much larger, groundbreaking science business."

Oh, right. That decision. Did I make that decision? Am I even here?

"But, most of all, you are going to adore the feeling of awesome, unbridled power you will feel when you finally realize all we are going to be able to achieve."

I would like to say that the phrase "awesome, unbridled power" has no effect on me. I would even more like to say that it offends me.

But that would be a lie.

"Awesome, unbridled power," I say. "Sweet."

Walking home, I am trying to make sense of it. I was sleepwalking. I sleepwalked my way all the way down to Dr. Gristle's office. For a job interview?

Power is a good thing, though, isn't it? Power, in the hands of a good person, put to good use, is an extremely good thing, one of the best things.

I'm a good person. Power and I will get along just fine. I will use power heroically, and be heroic.

I like hero Zane.

I walk into my room.

My room notices. I guess the whole power thing has gotten to me, because my vital statistics on the monitor are going ballistic. Temperature, blood pressure, going crazy. I'm sweating. I'm actually sweating enough that the wall is flashing a bright green neon ELECTROLYTE warning at me over and over.

My testosterone level is up.

"My testosterone level is very, very elevated!" I shout to the world. It is high enough for two people. It's so high it looks like I swallowed a whole entire bodybuilder.

"Next anticipated lavatory visit: imminent!" the JohnMon tells me.

"Don't tell me," I tell it back. "I know when I need to go —"

I guess I'm excited. I rush to the bathroom, get there just in time. I hope I haven't lost too much of that precious testosterone there. Judging from my saunter coming out of that bathroom, I think not. Nope, I think not.

As I step out, Hugo comes right up and starts sniffing all around me.

"You smell funny," he says. "You smell different."

"I am different, little man," I say, patting him on the head.

"Where were you?"

"Out there," I say, gesturing in the general direction of the world. "Out there in the big world, wheeling and dealing, making my way."

"Did you bump your head or something while you were making your way? Because you sound a little goofy."

"Ah, you wouldn't understand, there, little guy. But you

need to know you won't be seeing quite so much of me these days. I'm going to be spending my afternoons and Saturdays working."

"Working? Where?"

"Down at the veterinary complex. Learning the ropes from my new partner, Dr. Gristle."

Across the room, slumping in his cage, Alfalfa makes a loud noise more like a strangled chicken than a parrot. "Your *what*?"

"Partner. Well, I am working for him now, until I learn. But eventually . . ."

"This cannot be," Hugo says.

"Yes, it can," Alfalfa says. "I'm sorry, Zane, this is all my fault. It's because of the *suggesting* I keep doing while you're sleeping. I am sorry, I can't control it. But I am brainwashing you into doing all the wrong things. You have to get rid of me. Let me out and I'll fly out that window and never come back, I swear."

I really have to laugh.

"Heh-heh-heh," I say, walking over all manly to the birdcage. "You really think you have that kind of power?" I ask him. "You silly little guy. The truth is, I have never felt greater in my whole life. I have never felt stronger or surer, ever."

"See," Hugo says. "That proves it right there. Strong and sure? You? Zane, you once stayed home from school because you got knocked unconscious by hail."

"*That* was a freak ice storm," I say gruffly.

"*That* was a freak who wore a padded ski hat to school for the rest of the year."

Right. That does it. The bird is not making me who I am. I am making me who I am. Who I am is going to shock and awe everyone who sees me.

And I am never wearing a padded hat again.

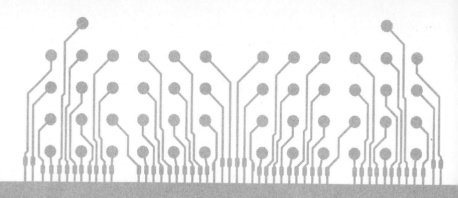

MACAQUE ATTACK

Zane, I need you.

I am out running.

That's right, running. I woke up with the urge and the surge, my muscles were all but bursting out of my skin, and I knew instantly that there was nothing else for it but to get out there and *run*. I feel like I am part horse today, like I could run long and strong because there is something beyond ordinary in my brain and in my body.

Zane, I need you.

It's my father, contacting me on the Gizzard™ that is strapped to my rippling biceps. I stop running, reluctantly.

Problem? I type.

Problem, yes. Need your animal talents.

I am probably enjoying this more than I should. But he is interrupting my run, just as I am about to achieve Mach 2. And it does feel like power, and I like power.

Details? I type.

He's uppercase serious. *MONKEY BERSERK! TER-RORIZING! GET HOME NOW!*

— ◆ —

Those capital letters don't lie.

I hear the monkey screech from two blocks away. As I step inside the door, it sounds like there is a blazing argument going on. That Voice is bellowing at Munson from within his office. Munson is in the kitchen, screaming back at my father and slamming things around.

This requires direct and decisive action.

I rush to my bedroom and lock the door behind me.

"What is going on?" I ask Hugo and Alfalfa.

"They're having a spat," says the bird.

"That's one irrational macaque you've got there," says Hugo.

That Voice breaks in over the ceiling speaker. "Do something, Zane. Whatever it is you do to get them to listen to you, please do that now. The vicious little monster has lost his mind."

"For starters, Dad, no name-calling."

"Oh, he can't understand me."

"You want to remain terrorized? They are a lot more sensitive than you think."

"Fine. Sensitive Mr. Munson has been throwing something at me that a respectable monkey ought not to be throwing."

"Snrff snrffle snrff . . ." Hugo can't contain himself.

"Zane, it sounds like that dog is laughing at me."

"Ah, that's just what he sounds like when he's got something in his throat."

"Ah hah hah hah hah," Alfalfa bursts out.

"And the bird? Zane, has the bird got something in his throat?"

"Not yet," I say, turning to Alfalfa, "but he might very soon."

"Please, son, take care of the monkey. I didn't do anything wrong, and he just snapped. I simply put some headphones on him for a promotional photo, and he went ape. You know, Dr. Gristle would like some publicity for the work he's doing, and it wasn't like the monkey was forced to do anything terrible. Anyway, he's crazy, and I don't want to deal with him anymore. Please help, son."

He keeps calling me son, which shouldn't be that big a deal since I am technically his son and everything. But it is winning him a vague warm sympathy just the same.

"I'll see what I can do," I say, and head for the kitchen.

"Good. Work your animal talents. Subdue him, then get him out of here. I don't want to see him again. Tell Dr. Gristle thanks, but we're okay just now for filthy neurotic screeching domestic help."

In the kitchen I find a deeply troubled macaque. He is chattering away loudly, angrily, in a high shrill voice that gives the impression he is making a passionate case against someone who isn't there. He is standing on the stove top. He appears to be readying himself for battle, with the stainless-steel pitcher from our blender on his head and a chrome meat-tenderizing mallet in his hand.

"You know," I say, standing a safe distance away in the doorway, "those blades on the inside of your helmet will probably offer more damage than protection."

He turns and bares his teeth at me. He's not smiling.

He takes the bartender's Viking helmet off, however, indicating he may not be crazy after all.

"Do you not like it here?" I ask, walking slowly in his direction.

He gives me the anti-smile again.

"Do you want to leave?"

I get no teeth. He is still holding the shiny meat tenderizer up like Thor's hammer — maybe he *is* a Viking monkey. A Vikey? His arm is getting tired, gradually lowering. His expressive face looks like when I tried to talk with him before, strained. He looks like he wants to talk to me, but is fighting it. Then he gives in.

"Ek edda ek edda yeeer yeer ekkeda . . ." and so on. Again it sounds like a whole bunch of speakers trying to get through on one feed and nobody making a shred of sense. He gives up. He drops the hammer at his feet, between two burners, and slouches.

His efforts seem to have exhausted him, and I'm feeling slightly drained by it myself.

Then he looks up. His face remains strained, but there is a steeliness in his eyes as he launches a series of gestures with his hands.

Munson points to me, then points to himself, then points to the door.

I stand there staring at him blankly.

He sighs wearily and runs through it again. With his right hand, he points his index finger at me, then back at himself. Then with his left, he points at the door.

"Signs?" I say, because I can just about keep up with a signing macaque if I concentrate really hard. "You know sign language?"

Munson, low on patience, picks the mallet back up and starts beating a savage angry tune out on the top of the stove in frustration.

Right, so it's not actual sign language, just kind of improvised.

"You want to go then, I get it," I say, opening the back door.

Munson drops the mallet, hops down, and walks calmly to the exit. On the way past he looks up at me and knocks on his own skull, making a coconut sound.

The variety and manner of animal insults I've received is strictly a tribute to the closeness of our relationships. I will continue to tell myself this.

"You should probably ride on my back or something, Munson," I say as he leads the way, walking proud and upright down the sidewalk. "People tend to get a little antsy when they see freewalking lower primates heading up the road."

Aw, rats. Yes, I realize what I said. And no, I do not know why I said it.

"Munson. Munson, please, I didn't mean anything . . . slow down."

I run after him, but he's fast. What happened to me? I was a horse just a little while ago. I still feel strong and quick and agile . . . but he's leaving me in the dust.

"Munson!" I call. "Please — I need you."

Good, good. I have reached that part of macaque where human and simian personalities overlap, because flattery now slows him down. Then he stops.

I run for a bit more until I meet up with him again on the sidewalk. He stands there expectantly. Waiting for flowers and an apology, perhaps.

"What?" I say. "I'm sorry. I didn't mean that lower primate thing — it just slipped out. From what I know there is no primate lower than man, and if you don't believe me, just watch. I will do or say something stupid in the next few minutes, guaranteed."

He's a tough sell. He stands there staring at me for a few seconds, wanting something more.

"What?" I ask.

He leans in my direction and taps his cheek with a finger.

No.

"You want a *kiss*?"

He hovers in that pose, tiny, yet statuesque.

Sheesh. I bend down and kiss his furry gray cheek.

The instant I do, he throws his arms around me and squeezes. We walk down the street just like this.

Affection. The miracle cyber-monkey just wanted some affection. Who'd've thought?

As far as I am aware, it is not take-a-monkey-to-work day, but I take Munson to work with me anyway. The boss notices.

"What is this?" Dr. Gristle says by way of greeting.

"This is Munson," I say. "You know Munson. You gave him to my father."

"They all look alike. How am I supposed to know who he is? Now that I know who he is, what is he doing here? He's supposed to be working for your parents. He's our prototype, high-profile ambassador of the WIP™ program."

Gristle sounds like a commercial. His front tooth sparkles for a second.

"They weren't getting along," I say.

The doctor goes all dark and ominous, staring at Munson. "Getting along? They weren't *getting along*? Mr. Munson's job was not to get along with anybody — it was to do absolutely whatever his master required him to do, and to look quite dazzling doing it. Mr. Munson is programmed *not* to have personality clashes with the master. He is programmed, in fact, not to have a personality at all."

Munson takes this opportunity to unfurl his dazzling smile in the direction of the doctor. It's not the friendly version.

"Oh, well, we won't be having this," Gristle says. "I'll be taking this monkey back right now, and I can tell you, when I'm through with him nobody will be smiling."

"No, Doctor," I say.

"No, Doctor?" he repeats with a raised eyebrow.

"I will work with him. I want the chance."

"Hmmm." His second eyebrow scales the icy rock face to join the other one at the summit. They suspend there for a few seconds, then slither back down again. "Well. All right, I suppose that would be a good project for you."

"I'll need a bigger office, though."

"You don't have an office, Zane."

"I'll need an office, then. I was meaning to ask anyway."

And just like that, my demands are met and I have an office. Gristle asks one of his Gristlies to take me to a room a long way down the hall.

"It kind of stinks in here, huh?" I ask Munson once we've settled in.

He shrugs.

"It does. I think maybe that'll be your job, to disinfect, since you are such a great cleaner."

My office is full of animals in cages. It is the holding room for animals that are boarding in the office for one reason or another. The doctor has a small desk shoved inside for me to work at — I'm supposed to be doing his paperwork and keeping an eye on the inmates while at the same time developing my own little side projects, like getting Munson back on track.

"Before he can be allowed to work with you," says Gristle, appearing in the doorway, "Munson must be punished for upsetting your father and for setting the program back so badly. I've just finished speaking with your father, Zane. He is quite traumatized, and flatly refused my offer of a replacement monkey. That is one very important man, and now we cannot count on his endorsement of our very significant work."

Before I can say or do anything, Dr. Gristle has crossed right over and scooped Munson up by the scruff of his neck. I would not have thought monkeys' necks had scruff, but he is dangling by it before my own unhappy eyes.

"What are you doing?" I protest.

"A day in the box," Gristle says, walking away from me. "Nothing less would suffice, and it is only because of your belief in this creature that I am not giving him much worse."

"The box?" I say.

When I say it, it causes disruption among all the residents

of the small cages banked up along the wall. Cats, dogs, and ferrets all start pacing, moaning, and slamming into the walls. *The box* does not enjoy a lot of support in the room.

It is like a large military footlocker, and it sits in the corner of the room, at the far end from my desk. With the protests of the animals and my own protests bouncing around the room, Gristle unceremoniously dumps poor Munson inside, slaps the lid shut, then spins the four wheels on the combination lock.

"That is barbaric," I say.

"That is tough love," he says before leaving the room and slamming the door just as unceremoniously. "If you really love a creature, you must be willing to put it in its place."

Munson is wild with rage. He flings himself against all sides of the box with such force that he must be doing himself damage.

"Munce, no, stop," I say, rushing to the box's side. There are several airholes generously punched into the top. I put my eye right up to one to try to see him, but I can't because it's too dark.

Then Munson takes his anger out on my eye with a furious poke.

"Hey!" I call, reeling backward and crashing into the cages.

"Seven seven seven seven," I hear in my ear noodle.

I turn around to find myself eye-to-eye — one eye, anyway, since I'm covering the other with my hand — with a chubby chinchilla.

"Hello," I say, since I do have manners.

"Hola," he says. "Name's Hector. I've heard a lot about you. Nice to meet you."

"Nice to meet you, too, Hector. What's seven seven seven seven?"

"The combination. For the lock. On the box. If you want to spring your pal."

"How do you know the combination?"

"He thinks we're furniture, so he does the numbers right in front of us. We've been waiting for ages to be able to tell somebody."

"Thanks," I say, and go right to the locker. Seven seven seven seven it is, and Munson is free. "Don't ever poke me in the eye again," I warn him.

He hops up into my arms. He's doing a squeaky embarrassing little monkey whimper.

"Ya big baby," I say, "you were only in there for a few minutes."

He is unmoved. It is only now that he opens up his eyes all the way, and I can feel him relax his grip at the sight of the light.

"You're afraid of the dark?" I ask. "You know, for a super-cyber personal assistant, you sure seem like you could use a personal assistant of your own."

He must take this as some kind of offer. He smiles — the friendly kind — then taps me on the chest with his eye-poker finger.

Great, now I'm an assistant macaque.

"You're running out of places to stay," I say as Munson and I slip out the front door. "But I know of a place, out in the wild, where animals rule themselves, and there are no people at all to boss you —"

He tugs at my shirt. He shakes his head.

"What, you *want* to be bossed around? If I were you, I'd have had my fill of human beings for a while."

He tugs again. Shakes his head again.

This is all he knows. He's afraid to live as his own macaque.

"We'll have to see about that, but right now we just need to find you a safe haven. Best bet I can think of is you mingling with your own guys. In a controlled situation."

He looks at me thoughtfully, and that's all he does. I'm not even sure he knows what I mean, but what does seem true is that he trusts me.

When we get to the WildWood, we find pretty much the scene we found before — a vast forest training camp for the Simian P.A. Academy. But what is much more obvious now is that the notion of cute little guys making tea and waxing cars is not the end of it. In fact, from what I can see,

I would be surprised if some of these beasts could even make a decent cup of tea.

All around, macaques are engaged in what can only be described as war games. There are several times more monkeys than were here before, and they are divided into squads. Each squad is led by one of Dr. Gristle's government goons. Each squad is precision marching, parading, blending, and unblending with the other squads like a choreographed military parade.

Except for the noise. There is no sound at all, no stomping feet, no barking of orders, no nothing. Each maneuver committed by each monkey is being ordered directly into their brains. The whole mass of them could descend on a town without anyone ever knowing they were coming. Yikes.

"Think you could just blend in there?" I ask Munson.

Munson squeaks.

"I'll take that as a no?"

He squeaks again.

I find myself shaking my head. "How did such a sensitive monkey as you even get this far? You were all wrong for this program, weren't you? Is that why you're mental?"

The squeak becomes a little more of a hiss and a snap now.

"Good," I say, "that's the stuff. Now listen, just go down there, blend in, do what the rest of the chimps do. It'll be fun. You can play army without really meaning it. They'll keep you, feed you just like all of the monkeys, and in a few days when I've figured out how to get you back in the house, I'll come and collect you."

Munson is not thrilled, but he's not biting or scratching me, either. We edge up close to the thickest part of the woods before the clearing. Then, when one squad marches near our position, I give him a little shove and he's in. In the group, and right in step. He's pretty good at this, too. Crisp marching, good rhythm, looking like he has been doing it all his life.

I leave him there monkey-seeing, monkey-doing, and I swell with the urge to pick up where I left off this morning.

I'm alone, and I feel power from that. I feel so much like I am a part of this right now, part of this forest, this WildWood, so much more a part of nature than the beeping and flashing life of my bedroom, which — while a perfectly great and cutting-edge place for a guy to live — has become a prison for me now, even more than when I was locked up for two months. I'm sick of my wall telling me when to go to the bathroom. I am sick of my father's magnificent voice booming overhead and shrinking me when I don't necessarily want it to. I am sick of my Newsmama's perfect head floating high above and telling me what the news is, side by side with her identical twin head asking me what I am doing under the covers at three in the afternoon. And they are both telling me with impeccable hair. Just for once I would like to mess it up, if I could ever reach it. And does my bath temperature always have to be just right? Maybe I'd like to get just a little burned once in a while.

I'm an animal.

That felt so good, just that, just saying it. I'm going to do it again.

I'm an animal, and I love it. I am running now, as hard as I can, through the woods, skirting the WildWater, as man-eating a body of water as there is, and I am thrilled.

My body feels like something real, fast and strong and springy, something with a purpose other than just a carrying case for my brain. What a feeling this is. Where have you been, feeling?

I run. I run and I run. I see obstacles ahead of me in the dense woods and I do not avoid them because it's a lot more fun to jump over things than it is to avoid them.

Why didn't I know that before?

I run faster, and trees are flying past me as if they are driving in the opposite direction. I run sideways to watch them better. I run backward to enjoy just a little bit longer the greatness of a stunning silver birch.

Bam.

I am on the ground, on my face, in the pine-and-oak musty smell that is probably just about keeping me conscious.

Great as trees are, if you run backward into them really fast they will knock you stupid.

I'm just stupid enough. There is an egg forming already right in the seam that runs down the middle of the back of my skull. It takes a little effort for me to push myself up out of the forest bedding. I pause briefly, to know I'm all right, and to appreciate the cool dirty smell. I'm all right, it's all right. I stay there on all fours for several seconds, enjoying it. I feel like laughing.

I howl instead.

Ah-whoooo . . . I call out, and I swear you would not be able to tell I'm not a wolf. I check my hands for hair before getting all the way up and running again. Just as hard, just as fast, just as happy and dumb.

I don't know how long I'm running for. Might be an hour. Might be a day. I never even get tired.

That's a lie. I *do* get tired, but the feeling of tired I have now is nothing like the kind of tired I tend to feel at regular intervals and for no particular reason. This tired here is a fantastic thing, not a negative at all. My knees feel like they could bend in any direction, they are so wobbly, and my thighs and calves are buzzing like electricity is being shot through them.

The only reason I stop running is because I end up reaching my destination.

The WildArea. I know that's where I am, even though I have never seen it before. Because I've gone way beyond the WildWater, out to the far edge of the WildWood, and fallen right out of nature into the wildest area I have ever seen.

Wild nothingness. As far as I can see, the earth is bald. If it is even earth at all. Not a tree, not a blade of grass, not a hillock.

It's sand. Fine, almost powdery sand the incredible deep color of blue spruce pine needles. It's like a blue beach lying nowhere near the water, not scorching like a desert, but cool, even misty. I can taste droplets in the air, sweet water that almost instantly quenches my runner's thirst.

I bend down and scoop some of the sand into my cupped hands. It feels like it's alive, gently pulsating like the grains are millions of tiny beating hearts. I hold on to it, laughing a little, laughing a lot, shifting the sands from hand to hand and laughing some more because the pulsations are doing something to me, to my own heart and my whole body. It's like the little hearts are synchronized with my big one, and the resulting hum of happiness is too powerful to resist.

"I know," says a smooth brown head that appears at my feet. "Isn't it lovely stuff?"

"Mole!" I say, and stumble forward to meet him.

As soon as I do, I sense a mistake. I begin sinking. Down to my ankles, my shins, my knees. I'm going down fast until I twist my body around and flop myself back up on what amounts to the bank of this sandy blue sea.

"A pleasure to see you again, my friend," says Mole.

"Pleasure's all mine," I say. "What on earth . . . ?"

"You're in the Zone, man. The WildArea. Bet you never expected *this*."

"That's a bet you'd win. Are all the animals here? All Gristle's experimentals, everybody got here, and this is where you live now?"

"Pretty much, yeah."

I see then, behind Mole, the giant terrapin poking his head up. He nods and disappears again. Then a fox. Then a seal. A salmon leaps up out of the blue, through the air, then swan dives back out of sight. Then a swan does the same.

"Mole, what's going on? What is this? Is this water?"

"It is what it is, man."

"Right. Well, everything is what everything is, but what I don't know is what *this* is, so could you be a little more helpful?"

"Yes. This, Zane, which you are looking at, is paradise. It's whatever we need it to be. If you burrow, like myself, then you burrow here. You swim? Then you swim. Slither, fly, run — whatever your game is, you can play it here because this here," he flicks some of the green-blue wonder toward me and it vanishes before my eyes, "is everything."

I can't contain myself. "I'm coming in," I say, standing on the bank and poised to leap.

"Sorry, my friend, but I don't think so."

"Why not?"

"I'm not sure why not. All I know is, this WildArea does not care for *Homo sapiens*. I've seen it with my own eyes.

You don't think the doctor and his goons have found this place yet? We weren't here for three days before they started showing up."

"Rats."

"Well, that's what I thought, too. Rats. But instead, we found out something good. Every human who tried to get in here lasted no more than seconds. They started sinking right in like you did, and some of them just barely scrambled back out. Then he came back with equipment. Weapons and tanks and masks for underwater survival and space survival and every type of survival they could think of."

"Didn't work, though?"

"Well, it worked for me. The harder they tried, the harder they failed. This body of whatever it is feels about humans the way Goth Sloth feels about jogging and polite conversation. All their gizmo stuff was completely useless. Nothing works down here, Zane, but *us*. You all are fond of calling this the WildArea, but we know it as OceanOrganic."

Mole has forgotten that he's not talking to just any *Homo sapien* — he's talking to *me*. And he couldn't know the changes that have been coming over me, making me more part of the team than ever.

"But this is me. Remember, I'm not one of them, Mole. Remember — you called me Our Friend."

"Ah, we love ya, Zane, but you're not one of us, either, now are ya?"

"Yes," I say, puffing up my newly expanded chest. "I am one of you. Something has been happening to me. I don't know if it's the chips and my intense relationships with the animals or what. But I'm experiencing things, feeling things, doing things that make it seem like I'm not entirely human anymore."

There, I said it. Thank goodness I have my good mole pal to confide in.

Mole makes a gesture. I can only see the top third of his body, and he is very small, but I clearly see a gesture.

"Did you just smirk at me behind that hand thing of yours?" I ask.

"Sorry," he says. "But come on, you are a sympathizer, and we all appreciate that. But you are a human, and I am afraid that is all you will ever be. We won't hold that against you, but we cannot lead you on, either."

My blood boils.

"Fine," I snap. "Watch."

"Zane, no!" Mole says and rushes forward in a frankly ridiculous attempt to hold back my power.

I am stomping forward, and down. Sinking again, I feel my heart pound, feel the amazing microscopic sand hearts pound right back. I go forward, go down. To my waist, to my chest.

I am truly petrified as I go under.

My mouth.

My nose.

My eyes.

Paradise does not do it justice.

I find myself in the middle of a multilayer world of swimming and flying and running. The whole of this world exists in a lighter-than-twilight blue-green. Everything is illuminated, fired by its own power so that every bird and tree and mountain is visible. It is a world apart from the world I have just left, a nearly inverted version of it, and I could not feel more at home if I were in my own bed. Not twenty yards away, a herd of small horses runs and jumps and fusses with a herd of sea horses of nearly the same size. I want to go with them.

I look down and see my friend Mole, looking up at me with astonishment on his squinty little face. Astonishment in a mole is just as unclear an expression as you would expect it to be, and a short while ago I would not have known it, but I am in a very different world from the one I used to know.

"See what I mean?" I say.

He just looks at me, still astonished, but silent.

"Well," I ask, "don't you have some apologizing to do — *oooh*ing and *ahh*ing, at least?"

Silence. In fact, everywhere is silence. I can see movement all around me, see life, feel it, taste it. But the only sounds are a kind of organic white noise.

Then I notice Mole go all panicky, scrambling and fluttering all around me and gesturing off toward somebody else to come over.

And that's the last I remember.

Until I feel myself bumping back up onto the shore, draped over the shell of the three-legged giant tortoise. It is a bumpy ride, and wakes me well up.

"What happened?" I say, rolling off the tortoise and lying on my back. I can barely get the words out. It feels like the tortoise has rolled on top of me, and twelve more just like him have rolled on top of him. My throat feels scraped and gritty. I cannot stop blinking my eyes, and if I hold them open for more than three seconds, it feels like they have been smeared with toothpaste. So I leave them closed.

"OceanOrganic didn't find you organic enough," Mole says.

"But I was there," I say. "I was there, and saw it and felt it and loved it."

"You know," Mole says, and he is right up near my ear now, breathing nice on me, "you were. And you did. We haven't seen that yet. Not from a human. Not even once. Oh, except for some human bones. We've seen lots of them."

I sit right up straight. "See, I told you. I'm changing. I'm not human anymore. I'm better now."

"Listen, I am but a mole, but I don't think humanity is something you can recover from. I don't think you can get *better.*"

I blink and blink and blink until my eyes will let me see the mole and the terrapin. "You, thanks," I say, pointing at

Terrapin. "And you, believe. I may not be there yet, but I can feel it, that I'm getting there."

Mole wiggles his pointy snout in a mole-version shrug. Then wends his way back to the OceanOrganic, allowing himself to sink chest-deep.

"We're all behind you, Zane, just like you've been behind us. But you might just have to settle for *honorary* animal. Our Friend."

I shake my head. "I have been there" — I point at the world behind me — "and I have been there." I point at the amazing world in front of me. "And I know where I belong."

"Right now, it's getting dark, and where you belong is home."

"I suppose," I say. "But I prefer this home."

"Okay," Mole says, "but what if you're wrong?"

I hold both hands up in the air. "I'm not wrong. I know I'm usually wrong. I'm at my best when I'm wrong. But I'm not wrong."

"With clear thinking like that, Zane, who's in the mood to argue with you?"

"Exactly," I say.

— ● —

It ends up that my parents are in the mood to argue with me. Oh, boy, are they in the mood to argue with me.

"What do you mean, you were out running? You were

out running? *You* were out running? You were out *running?*
You, were *out*, running?"

My Newsmama feels that running is out of character
for me. And no matter how many ways she bends the English
language, she cannot make the notion make sense.

"Did you read his odometer?" That Voice says from
high above.

They are arguing over me. Not arguing with each other
over me, because they are in complete agreement here. But
arguing over me in a physical sense, since Father is present
as the ceiling of sound pressing down on me like gravity,
and Mother is present as the well-buffed skull of televisual information beaming high on the wall. So, literally
they are arguing *over* me, but more accurately they are arguing *at* me.

Newsmama is working late on something and so is brit-
tle when she speaks.

"No," she says, "I have not seen the odometer reading.
Just a sec . . . oh, my. Zane. Zane, however do you explain
this? One hundred and seventy miles? Are you expecting
us to believe that you went out, ran basically all day, right
into the night, and totaled *one hundred and seventy miles?*
Your father hasn't totaled that much mileage in the last five
years."

I have to admit that I'm kind of stunned at the figure
myself. I have to admit it to myself, that is, not to anybody else.

"What can I say?" I say. "I'm a stud."

"Oh, stop it," she demands. "You are not a stud."

It feels like a small victory just getting her to say it.

"Stud," I say calmly.

"No stud!" she shrieks. And to illustrate what a cheap and immature little pleasure that was for me, I have to point out that my mother never, ever shrieks. Even when she reported on the launch of the *Narcissus 7* peace rocket to Tralfamadore and the liftoff fumes melted all the hair off of one side of her head, she finished reporting and refused to shriek until finding an offscreen mirror. So this is something.

"Zane," That Voice intones, "this is extremely serious, and we need a real answer. Do you realize you were not even trackable for a huge block of this afternoon and evening? Do you know what worry and commotion that causes?"

"Alfalfa seems to have left a few extra feathers under his cage, which is kind of sweet. But beyond that, I guess I wasn't aware. Listen, folks, I'm sorry, okay? But I was running. I ran a long, long way because I just discovered I love running and I am part horse."

"Part wha —"

"Figure of speech. I will be more considerate, if I have to. But I'm sure my odometer just went a little dipsy with the shock of me actually running and all." And with my visit to an entirely different reality, but why get bogged down in detail? "I probably ran about four miles. I think I'm going to join the virtual cross-country team at school when I can. And I'm starting to train for it right now by simulating real running so I can simulate simulated running better than everybody else. So, no more worrying."

"I'll stop worrying when you stop running one hundred and seventy miles in a single day," my mother says seriously. I look up at her on the screen, and she appears to be reviewing notes on another story.

"Okay," I say. "Next time I'll stop at one-fifty."

"Very good," she says, still reading.

"I think I see a blackhead on your nose," I say.

"What?" She looks up and all around and somebody rushes in and subdues her nose with a mighty powdering.

"Stud," I say.

"No stud!" she shrieks.

A two-shriek day. Am I on a roll or what?

When all that dies down, I am overwhelmed, in the relative silence, by tiredness. I wasn't feeling particularly nimble or complicated when I rambled in, so I ate the parts of my supper that did not require silverware — the beef burgundy and the mashed potatoes. Contemplating the baby peas made my head ache, so the peas went uncontemplated and uneaten. A five-minute shower followed by parental ping-pong has left me just about the strength necessary to fall asleep.

Hugo has beaten me to it. He is lying like a baby bear rug on the floor by my bed, and has been since I came in.

He is either asleep or a jerk, but either way I can't get up the interest. My eyes are falling closed as I take in the sight of the silent, sullen bird in his prison.

"Oh, for goodness' sake, open the cage," Alfalfa says wearily. "Open the cage, Zane."

I just do it. I have no resistance, and I stagger to my feet, toddle over, and open the cage door. If he told me to ball up and crawl in for a sleep on the cage floor, there's a good chance I'd have followed orders.

My eyes are closed before I actually reach the bed. I trip over Hugo and flatten out in a headlong leap toward sleep. I see, through my eyeskin, my room slowly dimming the lights, then snuffing them.

Alfalfa's bad voice — the creaky, creepy one — sees me through to unconsciousness.

"Monkey see, monkey don't," the creepy voice creaks. "Monkey see, monkey don't. Bad boy. Bad, bad boy."

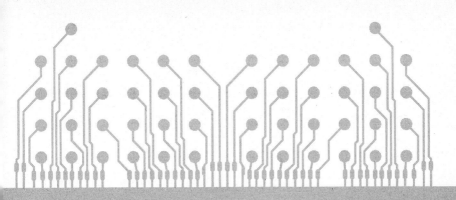

LUCKY BEAMS

I have the greatest life.

My dreams are becoming so incredible, I look forward to getting to bed early. Except that I get so excited to go to sleep that I can't get to sleep. Except that the wonders of my waking world are so great that I fear I might miss another something special if I'm sleeping.

I wake up stronger every day. I wake up surer and clearer, way more in touch with my animal side than before. And at the same time I understand better and better the big genius picture that Dr. Gristle is trying to assemble. I'm lucky. I know I am lucky.

"Good morning, Mr. Bird," I say to Alfalfa, the first face I see. I don't even mind anymore that he likes sleeping on my pillow. Who wouldn't want to be closer to a lucky chap like me? Maybe I'll give off lucky beams.

"Good morning, Zane," he says, and flies to the curtain rod.

I step over Hugo, who lies deadlike.

"How you doing, buddy?" I ask.

I am halfway to the bathroom before I click that he is not clicking. I turn and go to him. I get down on the floor and right up to his magnificent hairy mug. His chin area remains glued to the floor, but his eyes roll up to me.

"You okay?" I ask. "Everything all right?"

"No," he says. "Everything isn't all right. I am not right. I am not myself. And neither are you. I can feel it, Zane — it's all going wrong. We're losing, Zane."

I pop up away from this negative creature before me. Drag beams are probably just as contagious as lucky beams.

"Losing? I'm winning, my little friend. I am winning like I have never won before. I feel great. I can't wait to greet the next adventure because I can feel it in my bones that things are going the right way."

"Yes, so I've noticed. But while you have been developing your superpowers, I have continued to be a dog. So I can still tell when it's going to thunder and lightning, so it's time to hide in the bathtub, and I can tell when somebody is a danger, so I have to growl at him to protect you, ya big dummy. I know what your smell means, and I know that right now your bones are wrong. Your bones are, in fact, moron bones."

Strong stuff, I must say. Food for thought.

"Right, Hugo, you are coming with me to work today. The doctor needs to have a look at you and find out why you are so fritzy. I'm certain he will have something to un-fritz you. He's brilliant, you know. So you wait right here until I'm back from school, get some rest, then off we go."

"Righty-o," he says. "That's what I'll do."

His chin never leaves the floor through the whole conversation.

School passes in a blur, as school usually does. Then I run home, because running is a treat, and because I have to make up the time I'm losing picking up Hugo.

"Where's the dog?" I ask Alfalfa when I find my room dogless.

"The dog?" he asks, indignant.

"Come on, where did Hugo go?"

"I go go-go at the Parrot a'go-go."

Sometimes I think I understood animals better before I could understand them.

"Fine, talk gibberish. I have to get to work."

And that is what I promptly do. I start by doing the lame little things that are required at any animal facility. I clean the floor in the waiting room because a shocking number of pets cannot *wait* when they know they are at the doctor's. I log and stock all the feeds and beddings and medical equipment that's been dropped off by the lunks who drive trucks and have no idea of the monumental importance of our work here.

Then, when I've paid my dues with the grunt work, I go to my office.

"Hi, guys," I say to the unfortunate bank of caged critters who are heroically doing their part for greatness.

Nobody responds.

Then somebody responds.

Squeak. Whimper. Scratch.

I look to the chinchilla. "Is that . . . in the box? Is that Munson again?"

"Sí, señor," says the chinchilla.

I hurry to the box, dial in seven seven seven seven, and throw it open. Munson bursts out like a jack-in-the-box.

He wraps himself so hard around my neck I am sure this is what it feels like to be hanged.

"What happened, Munce?" I ask.

"When will you learn?" asks Dr. Gristle, coming into the room. He's like a bad genie who appears every time I rub the trouble lamp.

"I don't actually know the answer to that question," I say.

He decides to help me. "You think you can steal one of my important monkeys, stash him among my other important monkeys, and I won't find out about it?"

It didn't sound quite so stupid when I did it. It sure does now.

"Do you know what your problem is, Zane?"

"No. But it would probably help if I did."

"You are a combination of many great things. You have the enthusiasm of the boy and the complication of the man. You are a human with the senses of the animal. You are some percentage animal, but with the genius of . . . well, not me, but you get the idea."

"That's my problem? No offense, Doctor, but that sounds like a not-so-awful problem."

"Except that, all those things combined are deadly. What you need is the likes of me to make it all work. And since there is no likes of me, you need me."

Now I can see, that's maybe a problem.

"Well, I'm here, right?" I point out. "That's a start. Then when you pass on all your genius stuff to me, I'll be totally beastmaster."

Munson clutches me a little harder, like a monkey collar two sizes too small.

Dr. Gristle leans in and Munson leans away, making him a real pain in the neck. "You're already beastmaster, Zane. You have this uncanny knack with them that I have just not quite been able to work out. That's the part you need to enlighten me about, before we can earnestly consider attempting to geniusize you."

"Ah, go on, geniusize me."

"Heh-heh," he laughs. "Now, Zane, I admire a healthy ego as much as the next genius. Maybe even a little bit more. But you are suggesting some sort of . . . *equality* with me

119

while I am not only a scientific messiah for our age, but also, now, a televisual phenomenon. You, on the other hand, are a *kid*."

That was unkind. "You make it sound like a disease," I say, aiming to make him feel guilty.

"It *is* a disease," he says, dodging that bullet smoothly. "Fortunately, it is not a fatal disease, and you can outgrow it. That will take some time. But for now, you could just share with me your secret for animal empathy. How do you get them on your *side* like you do?"

It seems obvious to me. It's the same as anybody, right? You want to get them on your side, you talk to them. And you listen to them. And you care.

What if I just tell him? Maybe it'll be a wonderful thing? Maybe, if he unlocks the secret of my Gizzard™, he will be able to produce a generation of animal world translators that will change everything, everywhere for the good. Maybe I should just —

"Por favor. Por favor."

I turn around to see the chinchilla, his face squeezing like toothpaste through the grid wire of his cage. I give him a *huh?* look.

"Don't tell him. He's not you. Don't tell him, Our Friend. Nuestro Amigo. You are Our Friend, he is Our Fiend. Por favor, don't tell him anything."

"Zane?" Dr. Gristle calls me back.

"Por favor?" I say.

He raises an eyebrow. "Help me out here. Tell me the secret of knowing the animals like you do and you will have taken one big step to the kind of power and control and stardom we both know you crave."

We both know *that*? About *me*? That doesn't sound like me to me.

However . . . power and control don't sound half bad, either. Power and control are things I've never been in the same room with before. Power and control just might suit me right down to —

"Wait a minute," I say. "You were describing yourself. *That* was you who you were talking about, not me."

"Was I? You know, I suppose you might be right there. No mind, we can assume you have the brains and good sense to want to be like me, so it amounts to the same thing."

I walk briskly past him to the door.

"You know, Dr. Gristle, for some strange reason, I have been finding myself feeling *exactly* that way lately. Like I want to be like you. It's bizarre. But fortunately, there is a cure for that condition. Spending a little time in your company clears that right up."

"Zane," he calls as I head down the hall with my petrified macaque scarf cutting off much of my valuable oxygen, "we could be unstoppable!"

"Who would want to stop us?" I call back.

"Ach," he scoffs, "they're out there, all right. Don't get me started."

"I won't," I say, pushing the door open. "Bye-bye."

"You'll be back," he says smoothly, confidently. "Get a good night's sleep, and you'll feel better in the morning. And bring my monkey back."

I feel better already, to be honest.

"You're not his monkey," I say, peeling Munson from my neck to get a better look at him. "You're your own monkey."

He smiles. He can't fool me, though. It's a nervous smile, the kind you would call a brave smile if Munson were, in fact, brave at all.

WHAT THE CAT DRAGGED IN

My house, specifically my room, has always had something of a zoo air about it. Now, however, I'm actually *inhaling* zoo air. To breathe in my room is to taste the varied wonders of nature, and my health monitor wall graph has been edging up from *unhealthy* to *toxic* to *will not support human life.*

I smuggled Munson in under my shirt, and he's been living low profile mostly under the bed, to go along with my furry and feathered roommates. But this is where we tip over into beastly dense population of one bedroom.

In a shocking development, Hugo has gone out and retrieved the cat, believing that the resistance gene is now vital to everyone's continued survival. He is still lifeless and depressed, while the cat is . . . well, lifeless as ever, but authoritatively lifeless.

But here's the kicker. The cat has brought a pal.

"Hugo?" I ask as I step out of my slippers and into my bed. "Why are the owl and the pussycat looking in my bedroom window?"

"Because they are very curious creatures."

"Am I that interesting?"

"I sleep almost all the time in your presence."

He's wicked when he's cranky tired.

"Good night, old friend," I say to Hugo.

Hugo snores.

"Good night, Alf."

"Good night," he says from his unlocked cage. I eye for a second the slightly ajar door there, and decide I do not feel like running or flying or snake-slithering tonight, as fun as that can be. I feel like I want — I need — to merely sleep.

"Hey," Alf protests.

"C'mon," I say, "you could use a night off, too, and you know it."

He appears not to know it. "Rats!" he says as I push the door shut. "Puke!" he adds as I turn the key to the locked position.

I reach down beside my bed where I see Munson, wrapped up in a sweater and peeking out just enough to be out of total darkness. He reaches up and slaps my hand good night. I flop onto my bed and wave a friendly wave to the two spooky sentinels on my windowsill.

Funnily enough they do not return the wave.

I dream like never before. I am an animal, pure. I am like Pegasus, running like a horse, flying like a hawk, only way beyond Pegasus. Pegasus would cry with jealousy at my antics. I can swim, I can burrow to the earth's core and you know, when I get there it's not even too hot for me.

Brought to you by Dr. Gristle. Well, brought to me. Within my dream, I am not sure how or why, but in my dream he is responsible for what is happening to me. Like, he has personally attached my wings or something, but it does all come back to him, for which I am grateful. Who wouldn't be? Who wouldn't want to feel what I feel exploding in my chest right now? Who wouldn't want the chance to rocket into the sky at will just to look down on the beauty and inadequacy of the modest world way down below? Who wouldn't then want to bullet dive back down through that whoosh of atmosphere and punch a hole right in the earth's crust just for fun. Who wouldn't —

It's over. It's stopped dead. I have no wings. I do not breathe underwater or inhale the molten center of the planet. I just stop, the dream just stops. I calm way down and my chest deflates and things get all serene and calm.

And then I know. The doctor is vile. He is more dangerous than I could have imagined.

I wake up to a reality that makes my dream not so far-fetched.

Munson the monkey is marching. Crisp, rhythmical, disciplined military drilling, up and down the length of the room, up and down, up and down, grim.

I look up at my headboard and see the upside-down

head of Alfalfa the parrot, head comb at attention, staring intently at me. He's been talking in my sleep again. Then, next to him, right up against him, is the wildly impressive great horned owl. He has his head turned perfectly sideways like he's chewing the invisible ear off the parrot.

"And how do we feel this fine morning?" Hugo says. He's a bit more springy.

"What is going on?"

"Well, you've been the center of attention. Alfalfa was brainwashing you again."

"Yes?"

"That's where the owl comes in. He was brought in to brainwash the parrot into dirtying up your brain back to reality."

"How'd the parrot get out?"

"The owl released him."

I look to the cage to see that the owl has "released" the door clear off it.

"How'd the owl get in?"

"The monkey let him in, of course."

"Of course. Wait a minute. Is the owl chipped?"

"Nope, regular owl."

"So how's he brainwashing Alfalfa if he can't talk?"

Hugo lets out a great, dramatic sigh over my stupidity. "Oh, come on, Zane. Hello? *Owl?* He's an owl, for crying out loud. They can do whatever they want. They are bloody brainiacs — and don't they know it, too, with all the big-eye staring and asking you all the time who you think you are. If you stare at them too long, you'll wind up doing any old crazy thing they want you to. Especially you, with your weak mind."

"I don't have a weak mind."

"Hey, the stupid *parrot* made you think you were a superhero, and *his* brain is made of bread crumbs."

If there is a feeling that is the total opposite of the great power I felt at the height of my Pegasus dream, this is that feeling. What a chump I am. What a fool. I am still the same lame Zane I was before, and all the before before that.

"Thanks, Hugo, I won't let that happen again."

Hugo's feelings are a very, very, very small target. But sometimes I manage a hit.

This is not one of those times.

"Sure thing, kid, that's what I'm here for."

Munson, meanwhile, is still marching himself to oblivion. He's getting more agitated, and every time he marches down to the door end of the room, he pounds a couple of times, and does a little screech. Finally he comes up to me and starts tugging at me, pointing in the direction of out. He is so upset, tugging so hard I'm almost pulled to the floor.

"Think maybe we should go?" Hugo asks.

"Yup." I jump into my clothes and we rush to the door.

Just then, the most fearsome squawk comes from the bed, and I turn to see the owl showing us how impressive his wingspan and claws are. Chillingly impressive.

He lets out the noise again, flaps the wings a few times.

"He wants to come," Alfalfa says.

"Sure," Hugo says, "bring the kites, why not? Big day out."

We are barreling down the road as fast as we can, the birds flying high and far ahead, circling back occasionally.

It wasn't entirely a dream. I really can run. I am feeling it again. I lengthen my strides as I go, increase my speed. Hugo — serves him right — is having difficulty keeping up, and even the speedy little macaque cannot leave me behind. Eventually Alfalfa shows signs of tiring, while I don't even feel myself breathing hard. I feel like my lungs are the size of rocket engines and just as thrusty. Even the owl . . . well, no, I am no match for the owl.

We are in the WildWood. We are deep into the WildWood. We have come far, and we are still chugging, and Munson is driving us forward with a maniacal sense of purpose. We reach the clearing where the secret macaque training ground was, but it's deserted. We run and run and run.

We make it, after all, to the edge of the Wood, to the beginning of the WildArea and OceanOrganic.

And we see what the fuss was about.

The macaque army is marching all around. Silently bossed this way and that by Dr. Gristle's space-suited military menace pals. Munson, temporary soldier though he was, is receiving the same attack command as the rest of the invaders. Now he is panting, marching up and down in front of me with desperate pain and confusion on his poor little face.

And Dr. Gristle, puppetmaster king, is right there running the show.

"Hey!" I shout, then burst out of the trees in their direction.

The humans all turn toward us. The macaques all start coming after us until suddenly, without anyone saying a word, they stop and stand at attention.

"What are you doing here, Dr. Gristle?" I ask.

"And what gives you the authority to question me, young boy?"

"Those don't look like personal assistants to me at all. They look like little killers."

"Well, that's just a question of semantics, really. To someone who needs to do some killing, they are very handy personal assistants."

"Are you someone who needs to do some killing, Doctor? Aren't you supposed to be a man of medicine?"

"Oh, Zane, you have such a knack for putting things in stark, unpleasant terms. Things are much more nuanced than black/white, killing/not killing. The key here is to stay focused on the fact that we have all got to do our bit for the advancement of science, for the betterment of life on this and any other planet I might better."

"Okay, so why does that bring you here?"

"See, as I bet you already know, we, as humans, cannot go down there." He points behind him, toward the magical blue sand of the OceanOrganic. "No matter what we have tried. Whether we use underwater gear or space exploration gear, within seconds that *matter*, whatever it is, permeates everything — plastics, metal fabrics, human skin. It only accepts animals. Our grim, gray friends here just happen to be animals. But they conveniently share vital valuable traits with human warriors, such as gullibility, low self-esteem, questionable morals, and thumbs."

Munson has by now gotten so jittery I have to scoop him up and squeeze him like a baby to keep him still. From somewhere high in a tree behind me comes a shout. "Jerk!"

"Ah, I see you've brought along several of our old friends. I'm afraid their manners have suffered in your care."

Munson wriggles down, makes a maneuver, then throws something at the doctor that a respectable monkey ought not to be throwing.

I scoop him back up. "But what do you need them to do?" I ask.

"Listen, we are all aware how you stole so much of my very important work."

"They are Beings, not work, and you cannot steal something if it doesn't belong to anyone."

"We are all aware of what you did, and we are all aware of where they went."

"So, what, you are going to have your monkey thugs haul them all back?"

"I'm not sure how useful they will be to me at this point, Zane. I suspect you have ruined them for me. However, those chips they are carrying are hugely valuable, and crucial to my work. I need those chips back."

"So, one by one, the monkeys kidnap the experimentals?"

"I told you, Zane, I need the chips, not their hosts. The monkeys will retrieve the chips."

I notice now that each macaque wears a narrow bandolier, a little tool belt hung diagonally across their bodies from shoulder to hip. A little tool belt with vicious little tools that they have no doubt been trained to use.

"What's *wrong* with you?" I shout.

He sounds tired and wounded. "Is it so wrong to want to improve life as we know it?"

I wish he really was tired and wounded.

No command is heard, but the macaque attack commences. They spin, and begin the march to the sand.

"Man of medicine?" I shout as Gristle turns the other way to watch the proceedings.

"We all must shed a little blood for the greater good," he says.

"What blood have you shed?"

I watch as the macaques descend into the sand. Marching like machines, they file orderly down to OceanOrganic's edge, into the substance, down and down until their pointed ears disappear underneath. There are sixty macaques now, maybe even more. Armed.

Armed. How wrong is that?

"This can't happen," I say, and I march forward, carrying Munson with me.

"What are you doing?" Hugo asks, sticking by my side almost like a good loyal dog.

"I'm going in," I say.

"What are you doing?" Gristle asks as we stomp past

him and his faceless blobs of malevolence.

"I'm going in," I say.

"Oh, you certainly are not," he says, and laughs.

Several of his team also laugh. At least I think it is laughter. It sounds like guitar feedback.

When I do not slow down, he grows quickly unamused. "Zane? Zane, you cannot go in there. Zane!"

I am in. Up to my ankles, my waist.

"Zane, no!" he shouts just before I go under.

I believe I may have heard a tiny bit of actual concern in there.

Now I hear nothing. As soon as we are under, Gizzard™ cuts out. Chips mean nothing, and communication as I have come to know it with the Beings is off. I look down at Hugo, who is staring all around, mesmerized. He goes exploring. I get startled as, over one shoulder, Owl swoops by, followed quickly by Alf over the other. "Way cool," says Alf, the only other voice in this world.

The biggest difference, however, is Munson. He is still hanging on to me, but not nearly as hard. I feel his little heart beating wildly, rhythming to the billions of tiny hearts of the substance all around us. He cannot stop smiling. He squirms and squiggles to get down, and shoots away exploring.

Just as all his brother monkeys are doing.

It's a ball. It's a monkey ball, a Being Ball. Bandoliers are strewn all over. The intended victims of the intended massacre, rats and bats and moles and horses and all the rest, are mingling freely with the macaques, who have entirely lost their military ferocity and rigor. These monkeys are monkeys. And when about a dozen of them sail past on the backs of the giant sea horses, I feel a rush as good as any of my dreams and I know everything is going to be all right.

Which is just as well, because *I'm* not going to be. I feel the pressure coming over me, the sensation that the blue substance is getting in, permeating my skin and working into me. My lungs feel pressure from the center, pushing inside out.

I have to go, so I turn to go. I feel heavy, my legs freezing up, as I plod on up the embankment and make my way up the slope. I turn one last time to take it all in.

I can't help feeling the thrill again, with the greatness of what I'm witnessing here. The place where they belong. The place all the Beings need. The place where even a packet full of chips and a whole team of monsters are powerless to prevent monkeys from monkeying.

Then, Munson breaks away from it all, comes bombing toward me. He stands there, pleasantly slumping, no more rotten great posture.

Nobody can talk to me here. Probably for the best.

But Munson can talk anywhere. He takes the flat of his hand, and slaps himself on the chest several times while he points at me with his other hand.

I have to go. My lungs are hurting, and now my heart is, too.

"Me, too," I tell him. "Watch out for the dark, now."

Then he sees me off with that small gesture that started it all. He taps his cheek with his finger.

I bend down and kiss his hairy gray cheek. He wraps his little arms around my head, squeezes hard, and gives it a little bite. Just like real monkeys.

We both turn and go where we need to go.

I feel like a thousand-year-old man by the time my whole body emerges from OceanOrganic.

"Pressed your luck a little far there," Hugo says, popping out right beside me. Almost like a real, loyal dog.

"You didn't feel like staying?" I ask him.

"It's quiet down there," he says ominously. "*Too* quiet."

"Zane!" Dr. Gristle shouts, rushing toward me with his goon squad. "Are you all right? How did you do that? How did you survive? It's not possible to —"

"I'm tired. I'm going home."

Not that I'm not touched by his concern.

Then I'm really touched. By the goons.

Both of my arms are seized, and they just about lift me off the ground, spinning me to face the music man.

"Where are my macaques?"

This brings me great pleasure, brings back much of my strength and all of my wise guy.

"What would you do if you were a monkey? They're riding sea horses, of course."

He goes plum purple. It's a heartwarming sight.

"You should probably calm down before your head bursts into flame, Doctor."

"Do you have any idea the trouble and astronomical expense required to WIP™ each and every one of those hairy, smelly little beasts? If you can go in there, then you can bring them back."

"You can take it out of my pay, a little at a time, because I won't be bringing them back."

"Believe it or not, young man, there are people even more powerful than me. And they will be profoundly displeased at the setback to the WIP™ program. The loss of hundreds of very sophisticated chips, and highly trained beasts —"

"Beings. You mean to say *Beings*, but you keep stumbling over the word. I have the same problem. I try to say *genius*, and it keeps coming out *maniac*. You work on that, and I'll just be on my way. Come on, Hugo, let's go."

Hugo starts off, but I can sense from the grip on my arms that I have other plans.

"You have done it again, Zane, and you have done it worse."

I speak to the goon epaulets I'm wearing on each arm. "Guys, do me a favor and shrug my shoulders for me."

To my surprise, they oblige. One shoulder is shrugged almost out of its socket.

"Looks like some more house arrest for me, huh?" I say.

Dr. Gristle gets right in my face, breathing rancid fire all over me and scorching the joke impulse right off me.

"Playtime is over, Zane. When we're done with you this time, you'll wish you never came out of your room. And if you're smart, you'll never leave it again."

I think of Munson and try to put on a brave face. I'm certain it's no braver than his was.

But it will have to be good enough. Because this is not over yet.

End of Book Two